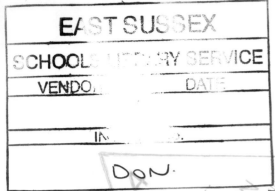

To the dear little men
HARRY DAVID and TAPIO

J.P.

To Mama and Papa De Salve,
with love

J.M.

Text copyright © Josephine Poole 1994
Illustrations copyright © James Mayhew 1994

The original story of *Pinocchio* was first published in Italy in 1882.
This retelling is based on E. Harden's translation of
Carlo Collodi's *Pinocchio*, first published in Australia in 1944.

This retelling first published in Great Britain in 1994
by Simon & Schuster Young Books
Campus 400
Maylands Avenue
Hemel Hempstead
Herts HP2 7EZ

Designed by Dalia Hartman
Typeset in Weiss Roman
by Columns Design & Production Services Limited, Reading
Printed and bound in

British Library Cataloguing in Publication Data available.

ISBN: 0 7500 1464 4

PINOCCHIO

Retold by

JOSEPHINE POOLE

Illustrated by

JAMES MAYHEW

SIMON & SCHUSTER
YOUNG BOOKS

The puppet is made, and comes alive. How he runs away to see the world, and has to beg for food, and comes home again soaked through. How he throws a hammer, and has a terrible accident.

There was once a kind old man called Geppetto, who made toys for a living. His home was in Italy. It wasn't much – just one little room on the ground floor of an old house, with a window under the stairs. What about furniture? He had one chair, a tumbledown bed, and a ricketty table – he couldn't even afford a cooking stove. That was all right! What would have been the point of it? He could only afford to burn scraps of wood, and he had hardly any food to cook. So he painted a dresser on the back wall, with its shelves full of food and drink. Then, when he was feeling particularly cold and hungry, he would draw up his chair to his little fire, and look at the painted dresser, and imagine what kind of a huge meal he was going to eat.

One day, a neighbour gave him a piece of wood.

"This is fine!" he exclaimed to himself. "This comes just at the right moment! For a long time now I've wanted to make myself a puppet – a dear little boy who will be like a son to me. If I'm careful, and use all my skill, he'll be able to turn somersaults, and dance, and leap into the air – almost like a living boy!"

The old man got out his tools at once, and started making the puppet. He thought, I shall call him Pinocchio. I knew a family of Pinocchios long ago. They were as poor as church mice, but they loved each other dearly, and they got along all right. That name will bring him good luck.

The old toymaker worked away, and soon he had finished the hair – the forehead – the ears – the eyes – but what was this? The eyes moved! They looked at him!

This was not pleasing to Geppetto. He thought to himself, That's a bold pair

of eyes. He said aloud, "Why are you staring at me?"

But as he hadn't made the mouth, nobody answered.

Now he made the nose. What a surprise! He made a nice little nose like a button, but it began to grow. It grew and grew. When he cut it off, it grew longer than ever.

He made the mouth, and what happened then? It burst out laughing!

"Stop that!" exclaimed the old man.

The mouth put its tongue out.

Geppetto thought, I'd better stop scolding him. When he's complete, I'll have to teach him manners. So he worked on at his puppet. He made the chin and the neck, the shoulders and stomach. He made the arms and the hands.

Now Geppetto was as bald as an egg, so he always wore a wig – a charming wig, of thick, yellow, curly hair. He was proud of his wig. He thought it made him look young.

Out shot a pair of wooden hands, and snatched it off his head!

"Hey! What are you doing? Give me my wig back this minute!"

But Pinocchio only laughed, and crammed it on himself. It was much too big. It covered his whole head, like a tea cosy.

This was too much. The old man's heart filled with sadness. "You've no respect, my boy," he said. "You're not

even finished, and you make fun of your father!" And he wiped away a tear.

But his work was almost done. He made a strong pair of legs, and fastened them to the body. Last of all, he put on the feet. Wham! He got such a kick, the spectacles flew off his nose!

Geppetto thought, It's all my own fault. I ought to have known he'd act like this. He's only a boy, after all! But he was as blind as a bat without his spectacles. However, he lifted the puppet off the table, and set him gently down on the floor, to see whether he could walk. Pinocchio's legs were very stiff at first and he kept falling over; he had to get along on his hands and feet. So Geppetto took one of his hands, and showed him how to put one foot after the other. The puppet learnt quickly, and soon he was running round the room, touching everything, knocking things down, moving so fast that poor old Geppetto couldn't keep up with him. Then, while his back was turned, Pinocchio noticed that the door wasn't fastened. He opened it a crack, and peeped through. Oh, what excitement! Without stopping to think, or say goodbye, he dashed out into the street!

By now Geppetto had found his spectacles, and he was trying to clean them; they were very dirty, and he was afraid they were cracked. At last he got them back on his nose, and looked round for Pinocchio. He cried out in

dismay. Where had his darling gone? Poor old man! He rushed after him into the street, wringing his wig in his hands, asking everyone he met whether they had seen him. He searched high and low, and vowed he would not go home without him. But Pinocchio was nowhere to be found.

The puppet hadn't had much of a welcome in that village. The baker had shouted at him for tasting a cake – just a taste – he wanted to see what it was. When he looked at the pies in the butcher's shop, a huge dog got up from behind the counter, and came towards him showing its teeth, as if to say, "Just try one – that's all!" So he helped himself to a peach instead, which made the greengrocer very angry, and he shook his fist and sent his boy after him. Luckily the boy was very fat and Pinocchio got away, and soon his quick little legs carried him out of the village, into the country.

Imagine being in the country for the first time! The wooden puppet was delighted with it. He scrambled through hedges and jumped over ditches. He explored fields, and chased cows. He ran races with a bull, and a gander. At last he was so hot and dusty, that he jumped into a stream. It was clear and swift, and there were little fish in it, much too quick for him to catch. When he came out, he rolled in the long grass to dry himself, and then he found a thorn tree that was easy to climb — being made of wood, he didn't mind prickles. He climbed safely until he could look out over the top of it. What a wonderful sight met his eyes! How wide the world was, and how beautiful! He stared all round, noticing everything, while his wooden heart beat fast.

But after a while he began to have a funny feeling in his insides. He couldn't put a name to it, but it made him say aloud, "How mean that man was with his cakes! He might have given one to me. I wish I had another peach!" He tried to eat some of the leaves of the tree he was sitting in, but they didn't taste nice. He thought, It's time to go home.

That was easier said than done! The sun, which had been so warm and friendly to him all day, had now rolled out of sight. Night was coming on; it was quite dark by the time he found his way back to his village. He was so hungry now that he could hardly stand. Geppetto was having a comforting bowl of soup with the butcher and his wife, and if he had looked out he would have seen his beloved Pinocchio stumbling up the street. The puppet stood outside the baker's shop and knocked on the door. The baker had gone to bed, but he put his head out of the upstairs window and shouted, "What do you want?"

"Oh please, kind sir, would you give me some bread?"

"Wait there. I'll be back in a minute.

– Beggars!" grumbled the old man, fetching a jug of water. "There's no goodness left in this world. – Are you still there? Hold out your hands!"

"Oh thank you, thank you!" And Pinocchio held up his hands for the bun he believed would be dropped into them. What a horrible surprise, when a stream of icy water came splashing down!

"That'll teach you to beg at my door!" shouted the grumpy old baker, slamming the window.

Poor Pinocchio tottered home, dripping wet now, as well as starving with hunger. There was nothing to eat at Geppetto's house, but he had nowhere else to go. He crept in, shivering miserably, ready with excuses if Geppetto started to scold. But the room was empty. His spirits sank as he stared round by the glow of the little fire basket – the only heat and light there was. At last, in desperation, he emptied the rubbish bin over the floor, in case there was a scrap of something edible to be found there. Oh joy! An egg! He seized it with excitement. It didn't occur to him that it must be a bad egg, or an addled egg, or Geppetto would never have put it in the bin. How to cook this lovely egg? was what he was thinking. He found a little pan and heated it on the fire, and then he cracked the egg over it.

Imagine his astonishment, when a tiny blue bird flew out into the room!

Well! He couldn't eat *that*! The bird flapped her wings and poised for a moment on the table. She cried out, "Thank you, my dear Pinocchio, for saving me the trouble of cracking my shell! Now if you'd just open the window – Thank you, my dear, and good luck!" And she flew away into the night.

Pinocchio burst into tears of rage and disappointment. He threw himself on the ground, and banged upon it with his fists, and roared and howled.

Presently he heard a little creaky voice which said, "Poor Pinocchio. I'm so sorry for you."

He sat up at once and wiped his eyes, and stared round the room which seemed to be empty. His heart beat pit-a-pat with fear. "Who's that?" he said, in a whisper.

"Only me," said the little creaky voice.

Pinocchio didn't much like the

sound of it. Now he saw that it came from a large grasshopper, or cricket, who was clinging to the opposite wall. It said, "Why are you making so much noise?"

"Because I'm so cold and so hungry."

"If you shut the window and the door, that will keep out most of the cold," the creature remarked in a reasonable tone.

Pinocchio realized the sense of this, and did as he was told, but he didn't much like being ordered about by a cricket.

"I'm still hungry though," he complained.

"Geppetto will be home soon, and he will look after you. He is a good man."

"Then he ought to be here already, making my supper."

"He had to go out to look for you," the cricket told him in the same serene tone. "Always remember this – no good will come to children who defy their parents, and run away from home. Sooner or later, they'll bitterly regret it!"

"You seem to know a lot for a cricket," the puppet muttered resentfully.

"Of course. I am a philosopher, and I have lived in this room for more than a hundred years."

"If this is as far as you've got in all that time, maybe you aren't as clever as you think!"

But the cricket was much too philosophical to be annoyed by Pinocchio's rudeness. He said calmly, "Tell me – what do you want to do with your life?"

"Me? What do I want out of life? To have enough to eat and drink, and be able to amuse myself, and see the world!"

"But first you must have an education."

"Go to school, you mean? Why? What for?"

"So that you can get on in the world."

"Nonsense! I don't see the point of that."

"Well, if you aren't educated, you'll grow up to be a great donkey, and people will make fun of you; and worse than that, they'll be able to do what they like with you!"

"I don't care! Who wants to go to school? It's a waste of time learning from books! It's learning from life that matters!"

"Poor, poor Pinocchio! I really am sorry for you," the cricket said in his tiny, grinding, creaking voice.

"Why? Why are you sorry for me?" Pinocchio was losing his temper. He wanted to thump that talking cricket.

"I'm sorry for you because you are only a puppet, and – what is worse – you have a wooden head."

This was all too true.

"What's wrong with that?" shouted Pinocchio. He grabbed the nearest of Geppetto's tools, which happened to be

a mallet, and hurled it at the cricket. It was the first time he'd ever thrown anything at anybody, and certainly he didn't expect to hit the creature. But unfortunately, he was a good shot. The cricket hadn't even time to give him some farewell advice – splat! There he lay, squashed against the wall!

The puppet was sorry then. He even shed a few tears. Alas – it was *too late* – the saddest words anyone can say! The cricket had made him so angry, he'd forgotten how cold and wet he was; but now he started shivering again. So he settled himself as close as possible to the little fire basket, and even balanced his poor frozen feet on the edge of it – a silly thing to do, but how should a poor wooden head have any sense at all? And he was so hungry, and cold, and miserable, and on top of that so exhausted, that he dropped asleep.

In which Pinocchio gets new feet, and a suit of clothes, and a book, and goes off to be the greatest scholar in the world!

He was woken by a bang on the door.

"Who is it? Wait a minute! Just coming!" he cried out drowsily, trying to get up on his legs, and staggering a bit. Crash! He went down with the noise of dozens of wooden spoons falling across a kitchen.

"It's your dad – Geppetto! Pinocchio! Is that you? Open the door!"

"I can't! I can't!" roared the poor puppet, bursting into tears.

"What's the matter?"

"Something has eaten my feet!"

"What nonsense is this," growled Geppetto, but he was so pleased to hear Pinocchio's voice, that he couldn't be really cross, and he managed to open the window, and climb in.

There lay the puppet in a flood of tears, with his little wooden feet burnt off!

"Oh my poor boy – my poor boy!"

exclaimed Geppetto, shaking his head, as he took three large pears out of his pocket, and put them on the table. "This is a terrible thing to have happened – and I was going to offer you some of my breakfast, but I don't expect you feel like eating."

"*Eating*! I'm so hungry, I could eat the whole world!" shouted the puppet, cheering up at once. And he snatched one of the pears, but the pear was hard and green, and he didn't like the look of it. "Why didn't you get me a peach?" he whined. "Peel the pear for me!"

"*Peel* it?" echoed Geppetto, in astonishment. "What's the matter with you? I thought you were so hungry!"

"I am, but I don't like skins."

So the patient old man peeled a pear, and another, and another, because the greedy puppet ate all three, and never thought that Geppetto had had no breakfast.

When he had finished, Pinocchio began to whimper. "I'm still hungry."

Geppetto pushed the peelings across the table. "Here you are!"

"But I can't eat *that*!"

"It's all there is."

So the puppet demolished the peelings, and the cores as well. After that, he felt strong enough to groan and complain because he had no feet.

"It's your own fault," said the old man.

"No, it's not, it's the baker's fault. He poured cold water over me."

"But you ran away from home, and got lost, and had to beg because you were so hungry."

Pinocchio was silent. He had to admit that this was true. After a while, he said sadly, "I'm sorry, Daddy."

Geppetto smiled at once.

"Daddy," said Pinocchio, after another silence, "could you make me some more feet?"

"So that you can run away again?"

"No, no, I won't, I promise!"

"It's easy enough to make promises, and hard enough to keep them."

"But I've been thinking about what the cricket said. He said I wouldn't get on in life if I didn't go to school. But how can I go to school if I haven't got any feet?"

"All right!" exlaimed Geppetto, beaming from ear to ear. "It's a bargain! I'll make you new feet – the finest that ever were made – and you'll go to school, and you'll work so hard, that soon you'll be the cleverest boy in the village! How's that?"

So he found a nice piece of seasoned wood, and set to work immediately, while the puppet sat and watched him – he hated sitting still, but he had to! And soon the new feet were ready, standing side by side on the table – two beautiful, nimble little feet, that might have been carved by an artist. Then Geppetto said, "Now shut your eyes and go to sleep!" Pinocchio did as he was told, and Geppetto fastened the feet to the stumps of his legs with hot glue, so neatly that the joints hardly showed. When the puppet woke up and saw that he had feet again, he leapt off the table and capered round the room, waving his arms and shouting with joy.

"Now," he said, "I'm off to school."

"Hooray!" cried the old toymaker, clapping his hands.

"But I've got to have clothes, Daddy," Pinocchio said, suddenly noticing his wooden sides.

Geppetto had no money to buy any. So he made him a suit out of flowery paper, and a pair of shoes from wood shavings, and a cap out of flour mixed with water. Then Pinocchio put on his new clothes and marched up and down, admiring his reflection in the window, and exclaiming, "Aren't I grand? Don't I look like a gentleman!"

"So you do," Geppetto agreed. "But remember – it's *clean* clothes, not fine clothes, that make a gentleman."

Pinocchio wasn't listening. Suddenly he cried, "But I haven't got any books!"

"What do you want books for?"

"To take to school! Everyone has a book to take to school!"

The toymaker scratched his wig, took it off, shook it out – sometimes he did find a coin in it. But today there was nothing there. He put it back on his head and thought for a minute.

Presently he hurried out, carrying his old coat over his arm. Pinocchio was beginning to feel restless without him when he came back, whistling, holding a shiny new school book.

"Oh thank you, thank you! You're the best daddy in the world!" cried Pinocchio. "But what's happened to your coat?"

"I sold it. I don't need it any more."

"But won't you be cold without it?"

"I can stay indoors if it rains. Besides, soon it will be summer!"

Pinocchio understood that Geppetto had sold his coat to get money to buy him the book. He put his wooden arms round him and hugged and kissed him.

Then he put on his dough cap, picked up his new book, kissed the old man once more, and set off for school. And Geppetto stood in the doorway of the old house, and waved until he was out of sight.

laughter, and did a handstand. He shouted, "It's a Great Puppet Show!"

"Oh! I must see that!"

"Have you got twopence? They won't let you in otherwise."

"Will you lend it to me?"

"Why should I?"

"I'll sell you my jacket."

"What's the good of it? It's only made of paper, it'll fall to bits when it rains."

"Will you buy my shoes?"

"What for – to light a fire with?"

"Well then – my cap?"

"No, thanks! The birds might peck it off my head!"

Now nearly everyone had gone into the tent, and the music had changed – the show was about to start. Pinocchio couldn't bear it.

"Will you buy this new book for twopence?" he asked, red with shame, but still holding it out.

His companion turned away. "My folks won't let me buy anything from other boys," he announced priggishly.

"I will. I'll give you twopence for it," said a junk dealer, who had been listening to the conversation.

So Pinocchio got his ticket and went in to see the show, while at home, poor old Geppetto was proudly imagining him working hard at school!

The play had just started, and Harlequin and Punchinello, two of the most important puppet characters, were having a fight on the stage. Pinocchio was entranced. He crept round the edge of the audience, and managed to sneak into a place in the front row. And of course, very soon one of the actors recognised him!

"Hey! Isn't that Pinocchio I see out there?" exclaimed Harlequin suddenly, interrupting the play. Punchinello dropped his wooden sword and stared into the audience.

"Yes, it is!" he shouted.

Then the whole company of puppets rushed on to the stage, calling, "Pinocchio! Pinocchio! Come to the arms of your wooden brothers!"

All this made Pinocchio terribly excited. He didn't stop to think – he leapt up on to the stage, and what a great reunion there was then! He was hugged, and patted, and kissed, and cried over, while the play was forgotten. So then the audience, growing impatient, started to boo, but the puppets didn't care. They were carrying Pinocchio shoulder high in a procession in front of the footlights, while he was shouting and waving his arms, quite giddy with excitement.

Suddenly, the Showman appeared! He was very very tall, and very very ugly, and he had a black beard that reached all the way down to his toes. He had little angry red eyes and a mouth like the snap of a letter box, and his whip, which he was constantly cracking,

was made of snakes and foxes' tails, twisted together.

When he came out, nobody spoke, nobody moved. The whole audience wondered what he would do. The poor puppets clustered together and trembled with a noise like teeth chattering.

The Showman glared round. He picked up Pinocchio by the collar of his paper jacket and carried him off the stage. The show went on.

The Showman hung Pinocchio from a nail, and no matter how much he struggled and cried, there he had to stay, because no more notice was taken of him. At last the performance was over and everyone went home, but the puppets still huddled on stage, anxiously discussing what could be happening to their dear friend Pinocchio, but too frightened to go and look. Suddenly they heard a roar from the Showman's tent – "Harlequin! Punchinello!"

The two puppets scampered off to see what was wanted. The huge man looked like a giant in the firelight, with his black beard and glowing eyes.

"Fetch me that Pinocchio hanging over there, and throw him on the fire! I'm running short of wood; there's hardly enough to finish roasting my mutton."

The friends stared beseechingly at the Showman, and wrung their hands, but when he saw their distress he looked so furious that they had to do what he wanted. They unhooked Pinocchio, who started kicking at once, and screaming, "Daddy, Daddy! Save me! I don't want to be burnt! Oh please! Oh save me, Daddy!"

Now the Showman *looked* perfectly horrible, but at heart, he wasn't so bad. When he heard poor Pinocchio's piteous cries, he suddenly burst into a tremendous sneeze. At this, Harlequin and Punchinello immediately looked more cheerful. "Courage, old boy!" they whispered. "It's going to be all right! He always sneezes when he has a change of heart!"

Poor Pinocchio couldn't believe it, and he cried on as loudly as ever.

"Stop that noise!" roared the Showman, when he'd mopped up his sneeze on a handkerchief the size of a tablecloth. But then he sneezed again. He said in a softer tone, "So you have a daddy, have you?"

"Yes, oh yes," sobbed Pinocchio.

"And a mummy?"

"I never knew her."

"Sad, sad," rumbled the Showman. "All right! I'll forgive you for sneaking into my tent, and spoiling my show, and upsetting my company. But I still want my dinner, and as it's still not roasted, I'll have to burn one of the others. *Harlequin*" he shouted, in a voice like a mountain exploding.

Poor Harlequin fell flat on his face at once.

But when Pinocchio understood that Harlequin was to be burnt instead of himself, he dried his eyes and stepped forward bravely, holding his dough cap in one hand.

"Excuse me, sir, but that's not fair," he said, trying not to sob. "It's all right. I'll go on the fire. I'll roast the mutton."

The Showman was so impressed by this heroism that he was overtaken by a violent fit of sneezing, and his handkerchief had to be hung up to dry. So nobody was burnt that night; they had a party instead, which lasted until dawn.

Next morning the Showman called for Pinocchio and asked him about Geppetto. When he heard how poor he was, his good heart was touched, and he felt in his pocket for money.

"Here," he said, in his growling voice. "Here are five gold pieces. They're from me to your daddy, with my compliments. You're a good boy, and one day you'll be a comfort to him. You can tell him I said so!"

Pinocchio couldn't speak for happiness. He hugged the Showman's legs, and the Showman bent down and lifted his dough cap with two fingers, and gently patted his head. Then Pinocchio said goodbye to everyone in the company, especially his dear friends Harlequin and Punchinello. After that, he set off for home, clutching the five gold pieces.

CHAPTER FOUR

Pinocchio makes two interesting new friends, and goes with them to grow money in Dupeland. Dinner and a bed at the Crab Inn. How he leaves in the middle of the night, and meets a talking ghost.

The puppet hadn't gone far when he met two beggars. One was a poor lame fox, and he was leaning on the arm of his friend, a poor blind cat. He was her eyes, and she was his legs, and so they managed to stumble along together.

"Good morning, Pinocchio!" the fox called as they approached.

"How do you know my name?"

"Oh, I saw your father only this morning. Trembling with cold, he was; I wished I had a coat to give him."

"Poor Daddy!" said Pinocchio, guiltily. "Never mind! When I get home I'm going to buy him a coat – a dark blue coat with silver buttons."

"Is that so," said the fox, and both beggars sniggered, the cat stroking her whiskers to hide her amusement.

"You don't believe me, do you?" shouted Pinocchio. "All right! What about that?" And he held out the gold the Showman had given him. If he'd been alert, he'd have seen the fox twitch the paw that was meant to be lame, while the cat gave the money a stare with her 'blind' eyes; but he wasn't quick enough.

"Well done!" drawled the fox. "That will certainly buy your Daddy a very smart coat – and several nice things for you besides."

"All I want is a new book."

"What do you want that for?"

"To take to school, to study, so I can get on in the world."

"Dear me," said the fox with a sigh. "I shouldn't do that if I were you. It was studying cost me the use of this leg."

"And my eyes!" whimpered the cat. "Don't forget my poor eyes! That was entirely due to study."

Just then a blackbird in the hedge twittered, "Pinocchio! Pinocchio! These are false friends – don't listen to them!

You'll regret it if you do!"

Poor bird! He had hardly a chance to finish his song, before the cat pounced and gobbled him up - beak, feathers and all! Then she wiped her mouth, shut her eyes, and went back to blindness as before.

Pinocchio was dismayed. "Poor bird!" he exclaimed.

"He needed a lesson. He won't interrupt again when people are talking."

They walked on for a while in silence.

Suddenly the fox stopped and said, "How would you like to double your riches?"

"What do you mean? How could I?"

"It's easily done."

"Very easily," the cat agreed, in a bored tone.

They all sat down by the side of the road. The fox said, "Listen. I'll let you into a secret. We're going to Dupeland."

"Dupeland! But I don't want to go there. I've got to go home, and give this money to my poor old daddy, and tell him I'm sorry for –"

"Shut up!" snapped the fox. "My dear," he continued more calmly, "don't you think it would be better to take him five *thousand* gold pieces?"

"*Ten* thousand," suggested the cat.

"Thank you, my friend – yes, even *ten thousand* gold pieces, instead of your miserable five? Listen then. In Dupeland,

there is a sacred field, called the Field of Miracles. All you have to do, is dig a little hole and put in – let's say, one gold piece. Then you cover it up, pour two buckets of water over it, sprinkle it with two pinches of salt, and creep away to bed. Next morning, what do you find? A marvellous money tree has grown up, and it is all covered with gold pieces! And they are all yours, my boy! You can take home as many as you can carry to your poor old father."

Pinocchio could hardly believe his ears. "What would happen if I buried all of my five gold pieces?"

"Why, five trees would grow up!"

"All *money* trees?"

"Of course!"

"But that would be heaps and *heaps* of money!"

"You'd be a millionaire," said the fox, standing up, and making him a sweeping bow.

Pinocchio's eyes were shining with excitement, and his heart was beating fast.

"But that's wonderful!" he cried.

"Wonderful for you! We don't tell everyone about it," the cat remarked.

"Well, I'll certainly give you a present –"

"Present!" the beggars interrupted, holding up their paws in horror. "We don't want presents, we do good because we enjoy it. We like to spread a little happiness in this grey world."

Alas! Pinocchio had completely forgotten the blackbird's warning, though it had cost that bird his life. He turned his back on his home, where his father was anxiously waiting for him, and taking the arms of his new friends, went off with them towards Dupeland.

It was a very long way. They walked, and walked, and walked all afternoon, and the two beggars leant more and more heavily on Pinocchio, until he had hardly any strength left. It was no good complaining, because the fox got snappish, while the cat had a nasty way of unsheathing her claws into his shoulder, if she suspected him of being ungrateful. Now evening was coming on, and Pinocchio was so tired, he really thought he would fall down and go to sleep in the road.

At last they came to an inn. A picture of a scarlet crab hung creaking over the entrance; the whole place looked rather dirty and disreputable.

"The Crab Inn," said the fox, stopping and looking it over, as though he'd never been there before. "Perhaps our little friend would like to stop here for some supper, and a rest?"

"Oh please!" cried Pinocchio.

"I dare say you're tired; you're not used to the hard life we poor beggars have to put up with. Very well, but we must leave at midnight, so as to be at the Field of Miracles before dawn."

So they went inside and sat down at

he winked often at the fox. Pinocchio was too tired to eat much, and he asked for some bread and nuts; but the cat gobbled up a dish of mullets in tomato sauce, and then called for tripe seasoned with butter and grated cheese, while the fox ordered a casserole of game and poultry.

It was astonishing to see how speedily the beggars demolished the food – particularly the cat, who never choked on a bone in spite of her poor blind eyes, and helped herself three times to the cheese, without spilling a crumb! Pinocchio sat yawning and nibbling at his bread, until the landlord took him to a dark little room which had an unmade bed in it, and here he lay down to rest. But sleep wouldn't come – only images of trees, trees with bright branches all covered with pieces of gold. The only trouble was that as fast as he tried to pick the glittering coins, they melted away in his hands!

He was roused by a violent knock on the door. He jumped off the bed – the innkeeper had come to tell him that it was midnight.

"Have you woken my friends?" he asked.

"Oh, they left hours ago! The cat had bad news – her son was took sick with the collywobbles – they had to go home in a hurry. But they said to tell you they'll be at the Field of Miracles, they'll meet you there at sunrise."

a large, dirty table, and presently the landlord appeared, wiping his hands on his grubby apron. The crab on the inn sign might have been a portrait of him. He was bald, with a scarlet nose and big scarlet hands, and little stony eyes which

"Did they pay for their supper?"

"Dear me, no," said the landlord, grinning, and scratching his bald head with his claw. "I understood it was your party!"

So Pinocchio had to give him one of his gold pieces, and he didn't get any change.

It was black dark outside, for there was no moon, nor any stars in the sky. Not a single light showed in that deserted country. Pinocchio had to grope his way along. His pattering feet were the only sound in the night. Occasionally, a bird flew silently across his path, and brushed him with its wing. Then he would start back in terror, crying, "What's that? Who's there?" But the only answer he got was the echo from the distant hills. "What's that —at —at? Who's there —ere —ere?" So he would catch his breath, and go bravely on.

By and by he noticed, as he walked, a faint little glow on his right, that moved as he moved. It was just a tiny comforting glow, and he wondered what it could be.

"I am the ghost of the talking cricket," a small hollow creaky voice replied at once, as if he had spoken aloud.

The puppet trembled with guilt and fear. "What do you want?" he asked nervously.

"Pinocchio, I want you to take my advice. Go home now and give those four gold pieces to your father. He's so unhappy without you."

"Of course I'll go home, but first I'm going to the Field of Miracles."

"There's no such place!"

"That's what you think – they don't tell everyone about it! I'm going to the Field of Miracles and I'm going to plant a money tree."

"There's no such thing!"

"You're wrong, you're wrong! It's a tree all covered with money, and I can take as much as I like, and I'll give it all to my daddy – he'll be rich and happy then!"

"You're talking nonsense, my boy."

"You won't say that when my pockets are full of gold!"

"Your head is full of silliness. Pinocchio, please – for the last time listen to me, and go home!"

"Stop fussing – I know what I'm doing!"

"Indeed you don't, and soon you'll bitterly regret it! Well, if you must do exactly what you want, and won't listen to advice, you'll have to take the consequences. Hey ho! Why should I worry about the ways of the world? Goodbye for the present, and may heaven protect you from thieves and murderers!"

With these solemn words, the ghostly cricket vanished – as abruptly as if he'd blown himself out; and Pinocchio was alone once more.

In which the puppet is set upon by thieves and murderers, and has to run for his life. How he is caught, and hung in a tree.

The puppet felt more cheerful after this conversation. He felt he had stood up well to the cautious old philosopher. He went on boldly for a while, wondering how far he still had to go, and how soon it would be sunrise. The night seemed as dark as ever. Suddenly he thought he heard a rustling, a scuffling on the road behind him. He stopped dead, and his heart began to thump.

Turning his head, he saw two frightful figures disguised in black sacks creeping up behind him, so close that he had no chance to get away. It's the thieves and murderers the cricket was talking about, he thought desperately — what shall I do with my money? Quick as lightning he slipped the four gold pieces into his mouth and hid them under his tongue. Next moment he was seized by the arms and two bloodthirsty voices roared, "Your money or your life!"

Pinocchio didn't dare to speak for fear of swallowing the coins. He shrugged his shoulders and spread out his hands, as if to say that he had none. But the robbers didn't believe him. Their eyes glittered savagely through holes cut in the tops of the sacks.

"That's enough!" snarled one. "Hand over the lolly!"

The puppet could only shake his head, and spread out his empty hands as before.

"We know you've got it!" squealed the other. "Give it here, or it'll be the worse for you!"

"And your father," sneered the first, with a horrible laugh. "When we've finished with you, we'll blow his head off!"

"No, no — not my poor daddy!" shrieked Pinocchio without thinking. He didn't swallow the gold pieces, but they clinked in his mouth, and the

robbers heard them at once.

"Ha, ha! So *that's* where the gold's hidden! Spit it out, will you!" cried the largest, slapping the puppet on the shoulders, so that he started to cough. But he shut his mouth tight, and he wouldn't open it, no matter what they did. He kept it clamped shut like a nutcracker.

So they rolled him and thumped him and kicked him and punched him, but he fought back fiercely with his wooden feet and fists. Then one of the thieves lost an ear in the struggle. When this happened, such a howl went up that Pinocchio was able to wriggle free and dash away. He thought he had a good chance of escaping, but glancing round he was dismayed to see the two robbers, still in their sacks, leaping and bounding after him. So he ran on and on, with his heart beating like a sledge-hammer.

At last he saw a tall pine tree just ahead of him, and he jumped up into it, and climbed hand over hand, right to the very top. This time he was sure he had defeated his enemies, but they were more cunning and more wicked than he expected. They lit a fire at the bottom of the tree, which soon flared up like a torch, spitting and popping like crackers at Christmas. Poor Pinocchio! He clung to the topmost branches, while the tree blazed beneath him in the wind, and the two robbers danced round the fire, waiting for him to tumble down into their clutches. Never! thought he to himself, and, "Courage!" he shouted aloud. He hurled himself out of the tree, and the friendly wind caught him by his paper jacket, and whirled him away, and set him gently down upon the ground.

Now he believed he was safe, but alas! The robbers had heard his brave shout, and they had seen him fly like a kite from the top of the tree. The poor puppet had hardly time to draw breath, before he was running once more – running for his life with those two horrible sacks close behind him. He came to a ditch full of dirty water, and thought his end had come – "Courage!" he shouted again, and jumped safely over.

But his pursuers misjudged the distance, and – Swash! Splosh! they fell plump into the ditch. That should have been the end of them, but no such luck! They struggled out and bounded on, dripping water like two leaky buckets.

Pinocchio had gained a little time, however, and dawn was coming, the blackness of the night was fading to shades of grey. A wood could now be seen ahead, and he thought, I could lose the robbers in that wood, I could dodge them among the trees. So he sped on, and as he entered the wood, he saw a little white house in the distance. I might be safe there, he thought. And he dashed on.

The robbers saw him run into the wood, and they guessed he would go to the cottage for help. They weren't able to catch him before he reached it, so they hid behind a tree and waited. He banged on the door which was locked. "Let me in, let me in!" he cried. "Oh have pity on a poor puppet who is being chased by thieves and murderers!" He hammered on the door again. The worst of it was, that he knew there was someone in the house. He could see a beautiful girl, standing in the middle of one of the rooms. Her eyes were closed and her face was very pale, and she had long blue hair.

"Let me in – oh please, let me in!" he shouted, desperately. But she wouldn't come to the door. And now the thieves jumped out on him, their cruel hands gripped him by the shoulders and shook him until he thought he would fall to bits.

"Open up! Open up!" they cried. But the puppet would not. Then they pulled out two knives, and that frightened him. But his wood was so hard, that the knives were useless. The steel blades shattered, without doing him any harm.

"All right!" snarled the big one. "We know your sort! We're going to hang you from that tree over there. Then, when you're quite dead, we'll easily get your money!"

So they put a rope round his neck,

and hung him from the branch of an oak tree.

Then they sat in their sacks on the grass, and waited for him to die.

Pinocchio was not very comfortable, and at first he wanted to weep, and give up his four gold pieces. But then he thought, Why should they be rewarded for their wickedness? I'm not dead yet; and he imagined the splendid coat he was going to buy for his father, and hummed quietly to himself to keep up his spirits.

After an hour or so, it started to rain, and the thieves grew impatient. They had snares to look at, and other evil business in the country round about. So they left the puppet hanging from the branch and went away, first telling him that they would come back in the afternoon, when they were sure he would be absolutely dead.

CHAPTER SIX

How Pinocchio is rescued by a dog dressed in velvet and a coach drawn by mice. He is visited by three doctors, and cured by a fairy with blue hair. How he grows a long nose, to his shame. How he wishes to live with the fairy and be perfectly good always.

Then followed a very bad time for Pinocchio. It rained harder and harder, so that he was drenched through, and a stormy north wind began to blow, that clattered his poor little body against the oak. The rope was so tight round his neck that he couldn't breathe, and he hurt all over. At last he believed that the thieves were right, and that he was going to die; so he shut his eyes, and gave up all hope of rescue. His last thoughts were of his poor father, whom now he did not expect to see again; and so the poor little fellow lost consciousness, while the chilly rain poured down, and the north wind banged him mercilessly against the tree.

Now the beautiful girl with long blue hair had come back to life in the little house where Pinocchio had begged so desperately for help. She was a fairy who had lived in that wood for more than a thousand years, and when she opened her eyes and looked out of the window, she was very distressed to see the poor puppet dangling from the oak tree. She leant out and clapped her hands three times, and immediately a blue bird flew up out of the wood, and perched on the sill.

"Do you see that poor boy hanging by the neck over there? Fly quickly and untie the knot with your clever beak, and lower him gently to the ground."

The blue bird flew off at once. She came back in two minutes, holding the rope in her beak.

"Well done! How is he?"

"I can't tell," said the bird. "He may not be dead, for I seem to think he thanked me, when I loosened the knot round his neck."

Then the fairy clapped her hands twice, and her pet dog marched in. He was a poodle, most magnificently dressed in a crimson coat and breeches, with large pockets for carrying the bones his mistress gave him at dinner. He had a velvet hat and a white curly wig, and he walked on his hind legs, in short boots and silk stockings. He even had a sachet, made of blue satin, to cover his tail when it rained.

"Hurry, Medoro!" cried the fairy. "Take the carriage, and drive quickly through the wood. When you get to the big oak tree, you'll find a poor puppet lying on the grass. Pick him up carefully, and place him gently on the cushions, and bring him back to me!"

Medoro wagged his blue sachet several times to show that he understood, and ran off. Presently the fairy's carriage swept past the little house. It was the colour of fresh air, with cushions as soft as daydreams, stuffed with canary feathers. It was pulled by a hundred pairs of white mice.

The fairy waited anxiously. Soon she heard squeaking, and the whirling of wheels. The carriage pulled up and Medoro leapt off the box, and opened the door with a flourish. There lay Pinocchio, pale and limp, his eyes closed, his face stained with tears, his cap and paper suit all sodden with rain. The fairy took him pitifully in her arms and carried him to a beautiful little room with pearly walls, full of sunshine. There she put him in a spotless bed, and she sang to him a healing song, but he lay still. So then she was frightened, and called three doctors – the cleverest she knew. They were an owl, a crow, and a talking cricket. They came at once, and stood in silence round Pinocchio's bed.

"Please tell me, dear friends," said the fairy, "whether this poor little puppet is alive or dead?"

The crow stepped forward and took Pinocchio's pulse; after that, he examined his nose, and his little toe. "I fear he is dead," he croaked.

"Rubbish!" hissed the owl. "He's as lively – as lively as an oyster!"

These two illustrious doctors always disagreed on principle, so that one of them was sure to be right.

Meanwhile the cricket crept up the quilt, and peered closely at Pinocchio.

"I know this puppet!" he suddenly piped in his tiny, hollow voice. When Pinocchio heard it, he opened his eyes wide, and quickly shut them again. "He's a spoilt brat, who's caused his poor father great pain and grief."

This was a hard way of telling the truth! Poor Pinocchio turned his head into the pillow, and burst into repentant tears.

The crow stared at him with amazement. "When a dead boy weeps, it's a sign that he may be getting better," he remarked.

"Yes, yes," hissed the owl. "Our ghostly colleague has cured him, without a doubt."

So the doctors left the room, arm in arm.

Now the fairy came up to the bed and put her hand on Pinocchio's forehead, which was burning with fever. She went to a little cupboard and mixed him a cordial.

"Drink this," she said. "It will make you better."

The puppet sat up in bed, and took the glass. He smelt it, and made a face. "I can't drink that! It's nasty."

"I know, but it will do you good. I'll give you some sugar afterwards, to take the taste away."

"If you gave me some now I might drink it," he whined.

So she held out a golden basin with sugar lumps in it. He took two, and gobbled them up, but then he wouldn't drink the medicine. "You'll have to give me some more," he groaned. "I can't stand the taste!"

"Very well, but you must promise to drink it," said the fairy, whose heart was full of kindness and patience.

Then he promised, and he ate more sugar, but he made all sorts of excuses, and wriggled, and cried, and all because of the horrid medicine, which he refused to swallow. At last the fairy sighed, and clapped her hands once, and said, "Look out of the window, Pinocchio."

He dried his eyes and sat up in bed, and did as he was told.

"What can you see?"

"I can see four black rabbits down by the wood."

"That's right, and what are they doing?"

He screwed up his eyes to see better. "They've each got a spade, and they're digging a hole."

"That's right, and what is the hole for?"

"I suppose it's a burrow for them to live in."

"Not at all! It's a hole to bury you in, because if you don't drink my medicine, you will die. It's very sad," said the fairy, as Pinocchio burst into loud tears. "But if you won't do as you are told, you must take the consequences."

Then Pinocchio begged for the glass of medicine, and drank it down in one swallow. And when he looked fearfully out of the window, the rabbits had shouldered their spades, and disappeared in the wood.

Then the fairy sat on the side of his bed, and held his hand, and he told her the story of his life, to the point where the thieves and murderers hung him from the rope in the oak tree.

"What a dreadful time you have had, to keep your four gold pieces!" she exclaimed. "Where are they now?"

"Oh! – I've – I lost them," stammered Pinocchio, turning red. Then as if it wasn't obvious that he was telling a lie, his nose, which was already rather long, grew suddenly two inches longer.

"You lost them after all that! Where did you lose them?"

"I think it must have been in the wood, while I was running to you for help." But Pinocchio blushed again, because all the time he could feel the gold in his pocket. And his nose grew longer than ever.

"In that case I'll tell my mice to search for them, for everything lost in that wood can easily be found."

"No! I'm wrong! I remember now how it was. I had the money in my mouth and I swallowed it when you made me drink your medicine."

At this third, colossal lie, Pinocchio's nose shot out so far that it pierced the opposite wall. Now he couldn't move in any direction without hurting himself, or breaking something. Once more his eyes filled with tears.

The fairy looked at him and laughed. "You'd better stop telling lies," she said. "That nose of yours will wreck the house!"

Poor Pinocchio turned scarlet with shame.

"I didn't mean – Oh dear!" What could he say, without his nose thrusting its way through the wall? "It's just – I'm

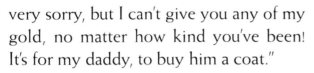

very sorry, but I can't give you any of my gold, no matter how kind you've been! It's for my daddy, to buy him a coat."

"I don't want your money, you poor little chap!" cried the fairy. "If you gave it to me, I wouldn't take it. But remember, you must never tell lies – never, never, never. That's one of the worst habits a person can have." Then she opened the window, and clapped her hands, and dozens of red and green woodpeckers swooped in. They perched on Pinocchio's enormously long nose, and pecked and pecked, until soon that ridiculous proboscis was reduced to its normal size.

"That's better, thank you!" said Pinocchio, as the last woodpecker squawked farewell, and flew away among the trees. "Oh fairy, I wish I lived here with you! I feel safe when you're looking after me."

"You can stay as long as you like. But are you sure you'd enjoy it, day after day, doing what I told you to do? That's what makes it safe, you know. Don't you think you'd get bored pretty soon, and want your own adventures?"

"Never!" said the puppet. He really meant it. "Oh no, I've had enough of all that! I'd be perfectly happy here, if only my daddy could come and live with us."

"Well, he can," said the fairy. "In fact, I've invited him, and he's already walking this way. He should be here in an hour or so!"

This was such wonderful news, that Pinocchio leapt out of bed with a shout, and danced round the room, jumping over the furniture and clapping his hands for joy, until he had to stop because he was out of breath. "Oh! I can't wait, I can't wait!" he cried. "Can I go and meet him? Oh! He'll be so pleased to see me again!"

"Of course you can, but mind you don't lose your way! Take the path through the wood, turn left at the crossroads, and you'll be sure to see him quite soon."

Pinocchio hugged her and kissed her, and then he dashed off, jumping over Medoro who was snoozing on guard across the threshold, running so fast that he had to hold on his cap with both hands.

CHAPTER SEVEN

The puppet sets off to meet Geppetto, but instead goes to the Field of Miracles with his old travelling companions. A glance at Fools Trap. How he plants his four coins and waits for his golden harvest.

The puppet followed the path among the trees, close to the big oak which he passed with a shudder. Soon afterwards, he stopped, because he thought he heard somebody pushing their way through the bushes. Could it be Geppetto already? No – it was his old travelling companions, the fox and the cat, arm in arm as usual, and very astonished to see him!

"Why, if it isn't our little friend Pinocchio!" exclaimed the fox, stepping forward joyfully to embrace him. "What a happy surprise! What a fortunate accident! How glad we are to see you at last, after waiting – how long did we wait for him, my dear, at the Field of Miracles?"

"Three hours," the cat replied sweetly.

"Three and a *half*, I think. No matter! True friends count neither time nor space, but only the value of affection."

"But I couldn't help it, truly I couldn't!" cried Pinocchio. "I was being chased almost to death, by thieves and murderers!"

"Never!" gasped the cat, ready to faint with horror. "What a world we live in! I suppose they stole your gold pieces?"

"No, they didn't! I was too clever for them!"

"Indeed," said the fox, stroking his whiskers. "Well done you! And now I suppose you're going to the Field of Miracles, to turn your four coins into forty thousand?"

"I wish I could," said Pinocchio, dazzled by this thought. "How wonderful that would be; but I can't today. My daddy's coming on a visit, and I'm going to meet him. I could go there tomorrow!"

"Tomorrow (as is so often the case)

will be too late," said the fox. "You see the Field has just been sold to a businessman, and he's already said he'll forbid anyone to trespass in it."

"But really I *can't* go today!" Pinocchio cried, distressed. "I haven't time to look for it, and I must—"

"Oh it's close, very close to here," the fox interrupted. "For that matter I suppose we might show you the way."

"Today is my day for visiting the sick," the cat reminded him.

"I know, dear, and I wanted to call on my old grandmother – never mind, our little friend needs us; come along Pussy. It'll only take twenty minutes," he continued, hooking his arm through Pinocchio's, "or perhaps half an hour – then you'll have planted the money, and tomorrow you can go and reap your harvest, and take your daddy with you. I see you've noticed her wound," he added in a lower tone.

Pinocchio had been looking sideways at the cat, who was short of an ear, and had her head wrapped in a blood-stained handkerchief.

"She won't want me to talk about it, but a word to a friend is not like publishing the story in the papers. Today we passed an old soldier, a poor wolf lying starving in the road because he had lost his pension. We had nothing to give him, of course, but my friend stopped. 'Cut off my ear,' she insisted. 'I have two, at least it will keep you alive for a few hours longer.' And so he did."

"Goodness!" said Pinocchio, impressed, but feeling rather sick.

"Goodness indeed," agreed the fox.

They walked for a long time – much longer than half an hour. At last they reached a city called Fool's Trap. It was a very dismal place, full of meanness and beggary. There was nothing beautiful, or happy, or good to be seen – only occasionally the sparkling carriage of an exceedingly rich person passed by, spattering the travellers with drain water.

"But surely *this* isn't the way to the Field of Miracles!" said Pinocchio, who was feeling thoroughly disheartened.

"It is only a stone's throw from here."

They went down a miserable, noisome lane, and came to a paddock where tussocks of grass and thistles grew, and rubbish had been scattered about.

"Is *this* it?"

"This is it!" said the fox with a grin. "Now, get to work – dig a hole for your gold – not too deep, or the pieces won't grow, but again it mustn't be too shallow, or some thieving rabbit will get it."

So the fox and the cat sat down and gave instructions, and Pinocchio scooped out the rubble with his hands. When the hole was dug to their satisfaction, he dropped in his four glittering bits of money, and covered them with earth.

"Now you must fetch some water from the stream down there," said the fox.

"But I haven't got a bucket!"

"Use one of your shoes, and make several journeys," advised the cat with a yawn.

It took a long time to water his money.

"What else must I do?"

"Nothing! We'll be on our way now; you must wait for the coins to grow. I daresay in about twenty minutes you'll see a little tree pushing through the earth, but don't be too hasty. You should leave them till sunset to be sure of a good harvest."

"I wish you'd stay – I'd like to give you a share of my fortune!"

However the fox and the cat would not, though he tried hard to persuade them. They strolled up into the city; but Pinocchio sat in a corner of the field, watching the sun go down, and hugging his knees with excitement.

There was an ugly parrot perching in a tree who brooded over the Field of Miracles. When the sun dipped below the horizon, and all the sky in the west turned a stormy red, he looked down on Pinocchio running with a beating heart to see how his money grew.

Poor Pinocchio! What did he find there? Not a sprig! Not a ha'penny!

The parrot let out a raucous cackle of laughter.

Pinocchio shouted furiously, "What are you laughing at, you moth-eaten old bird?"

"Flattery will get you nowhere," said the parrot tartly.

"Sunset, sunrise," the puppet muttered to himself. "I'm sure one of them said sunrise. I'd better spend the night here."

So he lay down close to his money, and the parrot tucked its head under its wing and went to sleep on its branch.

CHAPTER EIGHT

In which Pinocchio loses all his money! He goes to court to complain, and is sent to prison. How he gets out at last, and takes the road to the fairy's house. How he avoids a massive serpent; and suffers dreadfully from hunger; and is caught stealing grapes.

Pinocchio hardly slept at all, and when at last the pale sun crept over the skyline, he sat up feeling very chilly and wretched, with the horrible conviction that the money tree hadn't grown for him. He was right – not the smallest green shoot had managed to struggle through the ground!

The puppet wanted to weep with disappointment. The whole adventure had been such a waste of time, and now there was nothing to do but find his way home as quickly as possible, when he had dug up his unfruitful coins. So he scrabbled in the earth. He scraped and scrabbled more and more frantically, until he had a hole as big as a beer barrel, but never a glint of gold did he see!

At this point he heard a screech of laughter, and a jeering voice called down, "If you're looking for your four gold pieces, you're wasting your time!"

Pinocchio sat back on his heels and stared up at the parrot. Two big tears began to roll down his dirty wooden cheeks.

"What a fool you are," cackled the bird. "Fancy believing money can be got to grow, like cabbages and beans! Fancy trusting a fox and a cat, which are two of the most devious animals God ever made!"

"You mean they stole it?" said Pinocchio, with a sob.

"Easy job! While you was trudging down for water from the stream. Bless my soul! I haven't seen anything sillier since I was cheated out of my own tail feathers up there in Fool's Trap!" And he waggled the stump where his plumes should have been.

Pinocchio scrambled to his feet. "All right! I'll go after them. I'll make them give it back!"

"Not you! You'll never catch up

with them; besides, they'll have spent it by this time!"

"Then I'll tell the police, and you can come with me as a witness!"

"Who – me? Not likely! What would I say? Who's to care, anyway? It happens all the time!"

But Pinocchio ran back to the city and found his way to the court house, which was a magnificent building full of policemen, and officers of the law in grand uniforms. The judge was an old gorilla with a white beard and crimson robes, and gold-rimmed spectacles without any glass in them. He listened sympathetically to the puppet, and the clerk took notes in shorthand of dates, places and times, with detailed descriptions of the villains.

"I am exceedingly sorry for you, my poor fellow," said the judge, wiping his spectacles, when Pinocchio had finished his story. "Now, tell me what you think. Is two years in prison punishment enough?"

"Four," muttered the clerk. "One for each of his stolen coins. You can't do fairer than that."

"Excellent!" said the judge, and he rang a little golden bell. Two huge mastiffs appeared at once, dressed to look like policemen. "Take this unfortunate person to prison immediately," said the judge, pointing to Pinocchio.

Pinocchio gaped with astonishment, and then he started to shout, but

the dogs put their paws over his mouth, and carried him, kicking and struggling, to jail.

"What sort of justice do you call this?" he cried, as the jailer turned the rusty key in the lock.

"What sort do you expect in Dupeland?" retorted the jailer. And he went away.

——◦——

Poor Pinocchio spent many days in prison, and he would have spent many more; but it happened that the Emperor of Dupeland won a victory over his enemies. Then there were bonfires and banquets in Fool's Trap, and fireworks and bicycle races; and the Emperor commanded that all the prisons in the country should be opened, so that every rascal could have his freedom.

"Let me out," said Pinocchio.

"You are not a rascal," said the jailer.

"Yes, I am."

"Oh, very well, in that case," said the jailer, and taking off his cap, he opened the prison door with a respectful bow, and Pinocchio walked out.

It took him some time to find the path that led to the wood where the fairy lived. The mud was knee-deep, because it had rained without stopping all the time he had been locked up. But he didn't care; his heart was full of happiness at the thought of seeing his dear father, and the fairy again. He slopped through the mud and leapt the puddles, waving his arms, and singing a loud song. He travelled like this for several miles, without feeling in the least tired.

Suddenly, he stopped dead. There was something frightful lying coiled in the path, barring his way. He stared at it in terror, with his eyes almost starting from his head.

It was an immense green serpent, all covered in scales which made a rustling noise like dead leaves. Its eyes were like fiery marbles, and smoke gushed from its tail. Pinocchio did not much like worms of any sort – he was appalled by the size of this one.

He retreated to a little heap of stones, and sat down upon it, feeling faint. He thought he would wait until the serpent went away. He waited one hour – two hours. The serpent did not go away. It did not move at all.

Now it was getting dark, but he could still see the glow of its eyes, and the white smoke puffing from its tail. He wondered whether it would be possible to creep round it in the darkness. If it came after him – it would certainly cover the ground more quickly than the thieves and murderers in sacks! It would be able to climb trees far faster than he could!

Pinocchio imagined his father and the fairy, sitting together at her house, perhaps even now having a sad conversation about him. He longed with all his heart to reach them. At last he plucked up courage, got to his feet and, trembling in every limb, walked bravely up to the monster, who scrutinized him as he approached with its little fiery eyes.

"Excuse me, sir," he said. He was so scared that his voice came out in a squeak; he repeated the words. "Excuse me, sir, but if you don't mind, you are blocking the path. I don't wish to disturb you, but would you please be so good as to allow me to pick my way round you—" Here he stopped, because he noticed that the serpent had suddenly gone rigid! Its eyes were shut, the rustling of its scales had ceased, no smoke issued from its tail! Perhaps it had had a heart attack? Pinocchio couldn't help smiling – here was a stroke of luck! He stepped back a few paces, so as to take a running jump at it, and he had just left the ground when – hiss! puff! the huge serpent shot up like a spring, terrifying the poor puppet so that he fell headfirst into a deep patch of mud, and stuck there, with his legs kicking the air!

Fortunately, the serpent was not carnivorous. It was a harmless, humorous creature, and the sight of the puppet upside down in the mud struck it as so comical, that it laughed until it cried. But presently it moved to one side and kindly concealed itself; so that when Pinocchio managed to struggle out, he was very relieved to find it gone, and

went on his way quite breathless and covered in mud.

Now it was night, and he had hoped to be safely inside the fairy's house before dark. That couldn't be helped, but he didn't like it; he remembered the sacks, and the wickedness of his false friends. He kept up his spirits by imagining the great welcome he would have when old Medoro told the fairy that he was coming up the path. What a wonderful homecoming that would be! His wooden arms ached with longing to hug his daddy.

But he was hungry! And now the path wound over a hill which was planted with vineyards, and from the sweet smell, the first grapes were just ripening. He could see the shadows of the vines in the pale moonlight; he couldn't resist them. He thought it would be all right to leave the path just a little way, to help himself to a few grapes—

Alas! He gave a shriek of pain, and crashed to the ground.

Pinocchio had stumbled into an iron trap put out by a farmer to catch some polecats who were killing his chickens. He thought he would die with the pain and the shock of it. He screamed for help, but there was nobody to hear him. Only the moon looked down with an anxious face, and a firefly circled above him, like a spark.

"O firefly!" cried the poor puppet.

"Can't you do anything to help me?"

"What can I do?" piped the insect. "My poor child, however did you get caught in that fearful contraption?"

"I wanted some grapes, and—"

"Does this vineyard belong to you?"

"No, but I was dreadfully hungry—"

"But does being *hungry* give you the right to take what isn't yours?"

"No," said Pinocchio, in a small voice. Then he was silent.

CHAPTER NINE

How the puppet does the farmer a good turn, and hurries on to the fairy's house. The disaster that awaits him. How he is consoled by a friendly pigeon, who carries him on her back to find Geppetto.

Presently the puppet saw a bobbing light moving towards him up the hill, and heard the stamp of somebody in boots. He shouted, "Help! Oh please, please, help!"

"Ho, thief!" exclaimed a rough voice, and the farmer bent down, and grabbed him by the ear. "So it's you who's been killing my chickens!"

"No, no, indeed I didn't!" shrieked Pinocchio. "I only meant to take a few grapes!"

"Chickens — grapes — what's the difference?" growled the farmer, opening the trap, and tossing him on to his shoulder like a bag of corn. In this way he carried him down to his farm, which had a cobbled yard in front, where there was a henhouse and a dog kennel. The chickens were all shut up for the night, making feathery noises in their sleep. The kennel was empty.

"I'm going to teach you a lesson, my boy," said the farmer. "My good old dog Melampo has just died, so I hope you'll make a lively substitute, but if not, it'll be the worse for you." Then he buckled a greasy leather collar round Pinocchio's neck, and attached it to the chain which was fastened to the wall of the chicken-house. "Don't forget to bark if you smell a thief!" he said, and he went away, laughing heartily at his own joke.

Poor Pinocchio sprawled in the yard, half dead with hunger and fright. At last he crept into the kennel, and lay looking out at the moon. After a while, he imagined that he could see the fairy's face in that pale disc, and that her long, beautiful blue hair was hanging down, almost within his reach. She seemed to tell him that all was not lost, and that in spite of his mistakes, things would turn out well in the end. So then he cried a little, because he truly wished that he had been a better son; but still he was much comforted, and soon fell asleep.

He slept soundly, but just before dawn he was woken by low voices close beside him, and opening his eyes, he saw four lithe dark furry animals with prick ears and long tails, deep in conversation. These were the polecats that had been stealing the farmer's chickens, and seeing that he was awake, the eldest now approached him.

"Good evening, respected sir – what has happened to Melampo?" he whispered.

"He's dead."

"O sorrow, the poor beast! O alas! Shed a tear, brothers, for he is no more – the King of Watchdogs!" Then all the polecats sniffed and wiped their eyes and whiskers, to show grief; but really they were closely observing Pinocchio all this time, to see whether they could trust him.

"Then you, respected sir, must be the new watchdog?" the eldest politely inquired.

"That's right – it's a punishment," the puppet told them dolefully.

When they heard this, the polecats, being spiteful themselves, assumed that he would want to pay out the farmer for chaining him to a smelly old chickenhouse and making him sleep in a dog kennel. So they told him, in whispers, that if he would agree not to see them when they came once a week, and if he

would promise not to shout for the farmer, or make any disturbance, but pretend to be asleep – why then they would steal eight chickens, and he should have one of them, brought to him plucked and ready to eat!

Pinocchio thought it over. He asked, "Is that what Melampo did?"

"Melampo was our dear, dear friend," said the polecats, "a creature of unlimited courage and generosity." And their eight eyes glittered greedily in the moonlight.

Now the polecats believed they were safe, and one by one they slipped through a hole in the wall of the chickenhouse. But Pinocchio had already spotted a large stone lying in the yard, and as soon as they were all inside, he rolled it into the hole so that they couldn't get out again. Then he drew in his breath, and shouted, "Help! Thieves! Murderers!" with all his strength, but no one came. So then he shouted, "BOW WOW WOW!" and this time the farmer heard him, and stumbled out of the house carrying his gun; and that was the end of the killer polecats.

"Well done, my boy!" he exclaimed. "To think that you trapped those four wicked cats in one night, and my faithful old Melampo never caught a thing!"

Now Pinocchio could have told him about the shameful bargain between that *faithful* dog and the polecats, but he

didn't. He thought, I won't say anything – what good could it do? It would only upset the farmer. Melampo is dead – let him rest in peace!

He said, "They tried to come to an arrangement with me, and said they'd give me one chicken out of every eight they took, if I promised not to call you. Imagine trying to bribe me like that, as if I was a thief!" Then he blushed, remembering the grapes.

"That's right!" said the farmer. "Now we'll let bygones be bygones, and I'll show you how grateful I am." So he unbuckled the ugly collar, and gave Pinocchio some breakfast, and sent him on his way.

Now it was beautiful, bright morning with little clouds like rabbits' tails scudding across the blue, and Pinocchio ran along in high spirits. It seemed to him that the whole world was happy. Everything shone in the golden sun, and he remembered his own little room in the fairy's house. The butterflies danced for joy because soon he would see his daddy; from the high boughs of the leafy elms the pigeons cooed Home-home! Home-home!

At last he came to the wood where the fairy lived, and the sunlit path wound ahead between the trees. Soon he caught a glimpse of her little white house, and his heart began to beat fast. Come out, Medoro, you idle old dog! You must be blind and deaf if you don't know that Pinocchio is running, running towards you!

But what was this – what had happened? He stopped suddenly as if he had been struck. There was no dog on guard across the threshold. There were no faces at the windows, which were all shut, and the curtains drawn. The front door was bolted and barred – he tried it. It had a notice pasted on it which he couldn't read:

He sat down on the front step and looked about him. The carriage had gone. The lawn needed mowing, the flowerbeds were choked with weeds. Nobody lived here now, nobody had lived here for a long time. How would he ever find his daddy? He put his head in his hands, and wept.

Presently he was startled by a melodious voice calling down from the chimney, "Rain before seven, clear by eleven, rain before eight, clear late," and rubbing his eyes on his sleeve, he looked up. A large pigeon was sitting between the chimney pots, quite comfortably, because all the fires were out.

"Tell me, little puppet, are you crying because you have lost Pinocchio? Nobody knows where he is. The people here have all gone away to look for him."

"But I *am* Pinocchio!"

At this news the bird sailed down and alighted beside him. She was large – almost the size of a turkey.

"If you are Pinocchio," she said, staring at him first with one beady eye, then the other, "what are *you* crying for?"

"Because I have lost Geppetto, my dear Daddy," and the poor puppet started sniffing again.

"But I know where he is!" said the pigeon. "He's making a boat, to go to foreign parts and search for you. I saw him just three days ago, on the sea-shore!"

When Pinocchio heard this, his troubles were forgotten. He threw his arms round the bird's neck and kissed her.

"Oh, I wish I had wings like you! How far is it to the seashore?"

"It's a long, long way – but cheer up; if you want to go, I shall take you. All you have to do is climb on to my back – be careful not to fall off!"

So he did, and she spread out her wings on each side of him, so that he was riding on a wide raft of downy feathers. What a comfortable way this was to travel the world! He watched the patchwork of fields, woods, hills, cities as they passed swiftly below. If he felt cold, he nestled down into her plumage; sometimes he was so snug that he went to sleep. The sound of her steadily beating wings was calming to him. The

good bird flew all day, until it was evening, when she suddenly said, "Goodness, I'm thirsty!"

"So am I, and starving hungry as well!"

"Then we'll stop here a little while, for a drink and a snack. But we mustn't delay too long – I want to reach the seashore by morning."

Below them there was an empty dovecote. They crept in, and found a basin of clear water, and a basket of fresh green seeds. Pinocchio wondered what he would eat.

"You see how we are looked after," said the pigeon, when she had sipped from the basin.

Pinocchio said nothing; however he was so hungry that he tasted one of the seeds. To his surprise, it was delicious, and after that he ate them in handfuls, until the basket was empty. Then they set off once more, and he fell asleep very soon. But the good pigeon flew strongly under the stars, until a paleness lined the far horizon, in part the rising sun, in part the distant, silver sea. She cooed softly then to waken the puppet. She gently alighted, and Pinocchio, still half asleep, slid down on to the sand.

He had no time to thank her, or give her a kiss. When he looked round, she was already wheeling up into the sky, and soon disappeared in the brightness of the coming day.

*Alas! Geppetto has already put to sea, in the middle of a storm. How
Pinocchio follows him, and is nearly drowned, and comes to Activity Island.
How he runs away at the mention of a shark. His refusal to work. How he
finds the blue-haired fairy.*

Pinocchio had been full of hope, because the pigeon had promised to take him to Geppetto. But where was he? The beach seemed deserted, nobody was building a boat there, he could see no trace of the beloved figure in the curly yellow wig. However, he noticed some fishermen and their wives standing together at the water's edge, and he ran to join them.

"Oh please," he said, very out of breath, "I'm looking for Geppetto, who was building a boat on this beach – can you tell me what's happened to him?"

One of the men pointed out to sea. "That's him out there, but I doubt you can spot him, his boat is so small, and the waves are so big."

"He's searching for his son," said a woman. "We warned him there's a storm coming, and 'twas folly to set off on such a day, but he would do it. He's that desperate to find his child."

"But that's me! Here I am! Oh call him back quickly, before it's too late!"

Then everyone shouted, and waved scarves and aprons. But even if he heard, Geppetto couldn't get back. The tide was carrying him out to sea, and his oars were useless against it.

The people on the beach stared helplessly at the tiny boat. Sometimes they groaned, when a particularly large wave towered over it, but still it bobbed up again. Pinocchio's eyes ached from watching, but his heart ached worst of all. It was dreadful to see his father in such peril, and not be able to help him. He thought that perhaps Geppetto could see him watching and waiting there, because suddenly he caught a flash of yellow, as if he was waving his wig with a last message – Courage! But then – alas! – the whole sky darkened, lightning flashed upon the sea, and the storm broke. Geppetto's little boat could

be seen no more!

"I can't bear it!" cried Pinocchio with a sob, and with a desperate shout he hurled himself into the turbulent waves, determined – poor, foolish puppet – to reach his dear daddy at all costs. He was gone before anyone could prevent him.

In one terrifying instant, he was grabbed by that roaring sea. The waves reared up as tall as forest trees, and toppled over him with foaming crests. They caught him and tossed him about like a straw, and he lay in the water utterly at their mercy, for it was useless to try to swim, or even see where they were taking him. His only comfort was to think that Geppetto was adrift in this same sea, and any moment might throw them miraculously together. But the moments passed, and that didn't happen.

Pinocchio couldn't sink, because he was made of wood. All night he was battered and tossed, but towards dawn the storm subsided. He put his head up then and was much encouraged to see an island in the distance. It was no good trying to swim towards it, because the sea was still too strong, but he was carried closer and closer by the tumbling waves, until at last they hurled him violently onto the shore. Never mind! There he lay, safe and sound, and by and by the sky cleared and the sun came out. So he undressed and spread out his clothes to dry; and then he scanned the sea in all directions. But he could not find a little boat with one man wearing a yellow wig in it; There were several sailing ships, but all too large to be Geppetto's, though in the distance they looked no bigger than flies.

A sandy path led inland from the shore. He looked doubtfully at it. "I wish I knew where I was," he said aloud. "I hope decent folk live here, who don't hang boys on trees. I wish there was someone to ask—" As he said this, he noticed a movement in the water close by, and presently a large dolphin put its head out.

"Oh please," shouted Pinocchio, "I am a poor castaway on this island –"

"Come closer," trumpeted the dolphin. "Then you won't need to shout." He was a polite fish himself, and detested rudeness in others.

Pinocchio ran down the beach towards him. "Please could you tell me where I am?"

"You are on Activity Island," the dolphin replied.

"And is that a good place to be?"

"Very good – unless you are an idle waster; such people generally move on elsewhere."

"I have never worked, but I don't think I'll mind it – as long as it's the right sort of job."

The dolphin looked thoughtfully at him.

Pinocchio said, "I wonder whether

you've seen a little boat with my poor father in it?"

"Who is your father?"

"He wears a yellow wig and he is a small old man, called Geppetto."

"No," said the dolphin. "I'm afraid I haven't. But any little boat would have sunk in the storm last night – cheer up, little chap!" he said hastily, afraid that Pinocchio was going to cry. "I don't expect he was drowned – no, he'll almost certainly have been eaten by the immense shark which is spreading death and destruction in these waters."

Pinocchio turned pale, and moved back several paces. "An immense *shark?*" he repeated, fearfully.

"Rather! Imagine a five-storey apartment block – that's about the size of him, and then his jaws are so wide, you could drive a railway train, smoke and all, down his middle!"

Pinocchio was scrambling into his clothes. "Thank you very much!" he called over his shoulder. "It's been nice talking to you—" and he ran off as fast as he could, with his heart fluttering like a bird in case the enormous shark was coming after him to gobble him up.

He glanced back several times, but the shark didn't appear, so he began to feel more confident. Soon he saw houses in the distance, which must be the town the dolphin had mentioned. If they work hard round here they'll have plenty of money and bread, and won't mind giving me some, he thought. He felt ashamed to beg, but then he had to eat. The first man he met had a kind face, though he was worn out from pulling two carts full of coal, and glad to stop for a minute's rest when Pinocchio approached him.

Pinocchio spoke in a low voice with his eyes on the ground. "Please, sir, I'm so hungry, will you give me a penny?"

"I'll give you two, if you'll give me a hand," said the coalman, wiping the sweat from his brow.

"But I can't pull carts!" exclaimed the puppet. "I'm not a donkey!"

"Aren't you?" said the coalman. "Then if you're hungry, you'd better eat your own pride, and take care you don't get a pain!" And he went slowly on, dragging the carts behind him.

Pinocchio found a sunny place and sat down on the edge of the road. The next person to pass was a builder, carrying a bag of cement on his shoulder. Pinocchio coughed, and said in his meekest voice, "Please, sir, could you spare a penny for a poor castaway suffering terribly from hunger?"

"I'll do better than that," said the builder. "If you come with me and haul cement all day, I'll give you five!"

"But I'm not strong enough," objected the puppet. "I've had a long sea voyage. I'm worn out!"

"Then you'd better go back to where you came from," said the builder, and he went on his way, whistling.

There were plenty of people up and down that street, and Pinocchio begged from them all, but no one gave him anything except advice. "You should be ashamed to beg," they said. "Do some work – start earning your living! Don't you know that the bread you earn has the nicest taste?"

By now it was late in the day, and Pinocchio was burning with thirst. At last a tall young woman passed, carrying two pails of water. "Oh please, may I drink from your bucket?" he cried.

"Of course!" she said, and she put down both pails, and Pinocchio lapped like an animal. The woman watched him.

"Why don't you come back with me? I have bread and cheese and grapes at home; you're welcome to share them."

He looked up at her, and something in her face was familiar, but still he whined, "I'm afraid you'll want me to work for you, before you give me anything."

"You can help me carry my water; you can take the little bucket, because you are smaller than I am." She smiled at him, and added, "I made some cakes this morning."

Pinocchio could not resist the thought of the cakes. He followed her home, carrying the smaller of the woman's buckets.

Her house was plain, and very clean. The sun seemed to shine more brightly there than in other places. She sat Pinocchio at the table, and set some bread and cheese, and a bunch of green grapes, in front of him. He was famished, and ate like a wolf; he didn't look up until he had devoured every crumb; and then, instead of thanking her, he sat staring at her as if he was bewitched, with his mouth open in an O of surprise.

"What's the matter?" she asked with a smile, putting a plate of cakes on the table.

"But it's— Your hair! You look like— No, it is you! I know who you are!" he exclaimed. "You're the fairy, the good fairy from long ago – and I thought I'd never see you again!" He got up so hastily that he knocked over his chair, and clasped her in his wooden arms. "Such terrible things have happened to me!" he cried. "I've had such dreadful adventures! Oh please, now I've found you again, let me live here with you! Don't drive me away!"

"I won't do that." The fairy gently patted his head, and gave him a kiss. "It was you who went off before, remember! I'll keep you here as long as you want to stay."

"That's for always," he said, never doubting that this must be true. "I'll be your son if you like, now I've lost my poor father. Where can he be? Shall I ever see him again?"

"Oh, I think so," said the fairy, looking down at his anxious face. "Yes, I'm sure you will!"

Then Pinocchio beamed like the sun, although his eyes were full of tears.

After a while, he said, "You've changed – you've grown a lot since I saw you last."

"You haven't."

"I know. That's because I'm a puppet, isn't it? I wish I could grow. I wish I could be a real boy, and grow into a man."

"So you could, if you wanted it enough. But I'm afraid it would be very difficult for you."

"Why?" said Pinocchio, noticing the cakes, and scrambling back on to his chair. He went on with his mouth full, "Why should it be specially difficult for me?"

"Because you're so wilful, and impetuous. An idea comes to you – money trees for instance – and you rush after it, and never think sensibly about it, or anything else. That's why you keep getting into trouble."

Pinocchio wanted to argue, but when he thought about it, he could see that she was right.

"I don't see how I can change my nature," he said sadly.

"It really is possible, if you try hard enough. Cheer up! If you live with me, and go to school—"

"But I *hate* school," he groaned.

"Nonsense! You've never tried it. A bright boy like you will enjoy it, I promise. Then, when you've learnt a lot, you'll choose what work you want to do."

"But I don't want to work."

"But you can't live at other people's expense all the time! If you do, you'll stay a puppet: what else can you be?"

Pinocchio considered this, as he finished the cakes. "I suppose you're right," he said at last. "Well, I shall do it, if it's the only way to become a real boy. But it'll be hard for me – very hard – won't it?"

"Perhaps, just at first," said the fairy. "But I'll help, and then, when you see your daddy again, just think how proud he'll be!"

This was such a wonderful idea that Pinocchio leapt up with a shout, sending his chair crashing to the ground once more, and careered round the room, feeling as if he could pull twenty coal-carts and haul lime for weeks, if it would please Geppetto. So he went happily to bed, and next day—

CHAPTER ELEVEN

In which the puppet goes to school, and soon comes top of his class. How some boys make a fool of him, and they fight, and one is badly hurt. How Pinocchio is arrested for what is not his fault. How he is chased by a dog, and saves its life.

Next day Pinocchio went to school.

He was the only puppet, and the other boys found him exceedingly funny. First they tried to carry him about like a doll, and take his clothes off. Then one painted a black moustache under his nose, while the rest tied strings to his hands and feet, so that they could make him dance. Pinocchio bore it patiently for a while, but at last he lost his temper. "Stop it!" he shouted. "I'm not a toy!"

This made the bullies hoot with laughter, and the meanest of them, who had snatched off the dough cap to wear on his own head, reached out to pull the puppet's nose.

Ouch! He got such a hack on the shins that he backed off in a hurry! Then there was a fight, but Pinocchio lashed out bravely with his wooden feet and fists, and did such damage that soon the boys left him alone. They went back to

their desks, rubbing their bruises and glowering at him.

But he was so cheerful and friendly that as the days passed, they couldn't help liking him. The schoolmaster liked him as well, because he was clever in class, and worked hard. In fact, Pinocchio had just one fault – he wasn't careful enough over his choice of friends. Some boys were bad and some were good, but he got on equally well with both sorts. The fairy said, "Take care, Pinocchio! Surely you've learnt by now that false friends lead to bad trouble!" But he only laughed. The bad boys were often more amusing than the good ones, and he didn't see how they could do him any harm.

He was on his way to school one morning when he met a group of these not-so-good boys, who shouted to him, "Have you heard the news?"

"No – what news?"

"Why, there's a shark as big as a mountain – he's lying five miles out but you can easily see him from the shore! We're going down to have a look – why don't you join us?"

Five miles out – that was too far to be dangerous. Pinocchio had a sudden longing to see this monster, which he guessed must be the same as the one the dolphin had told him about.

"What about school?"

"What about it? We won't be very late – we can get there and back in an hour."

"We could see it afterwards."

"You dope – do you think a shark like that is going to wait for us? It's a biological curiosity, don't you realize? Come on – we'll have more fun if you do!"

That was an irresistible reason for going, and Pinocchio shouted, "All right! Race you to the shore, and the best man wins!"

Then they all ran at top speed across the fields, still clutching their schoolbooks, but Pinocchio ran faster than any of them, as if he had wings on his heels. He was first on the beach, but when he looked eagerly out to sea, there was no mountainous shark. The water lay as calm and undisturbed as a sheet of blue glass.

"Where's this shark of yours?" he demanded of his friends when they joined him, hot and dusty and out of breath.

Some of the boys started sniggering.

"He must've run away when he heard you coming," said one.

"I think he's burst," said another.

"That's right – I heard a bang," said a third.

Now Pinocchio saw that he had been tricked, and he said angrily, "Why are you trying to make a fool of me?"

"We've made one, haven't we? Fancy believing a tale about an enormous shark – and you think yourself so clever!"

"No, I don't!"

"You do! You do nothing but study!"

"Why should you care?"

"Because you make us look stupid. You'd better change your ways – or it'll be the worse for you!"

"You'd better listen to us, Pinocchio," said the biggest of the boys. "We're seven to one – you don't stand a chance."

The puppet laughed, and made a rude noise.

Then the big boy thumped him, and he thumped him back, and in a moment everyone was fighting furiously.

Although he was so outnumbered, Pinocchio was not afraid in the least. He backed against some rocks and struck out at his enemies, and did more damage than he got. This made the boys very angry and reckless, and they unbuckled their schoolbags and started hurling their books at the puppet. Atlases, grammars, dictionaries, mathematical instruments came flying at him, but he dodged so quickly that most of them missed him, and flew on into the sea.

Presently a hoary old crab sidled out of the water and called in a deep, hoarse voice, "Boys! Boys! Stop it at once! You ought to be ashamed of yourselves!" But nobody took the slightest notice of him, and Pinocchio called back rudely, "Go to bed, old croaker, and take some cough medicine!"

Then one of the boys noticed Pinocchio's school bag lying on the ground. He opened it quickly and shared the contents between his friends, keeping the largest and heaviest book for himself. It was a Treatise on Arithmetic, an antique volume bound in leather, which Pinocchio had won as a prize. He raised his arm and aimed it at the puppet, but by mischance it struck one of his friends instead!

The child turned as white as paper, and tumbled full length upon the sand. The bad boys were very frightened then, and ran away as fast as they could, in case he was badly hurt, or even dead. But Pinocchio wet his handkerchief in the sea, and spread it on the injured boy's forehead, and knelt beside him, rubbing his hands and trying to encourage him by talking cheerfully to him, though he was dreadfully afraid that he was beyond help. He could only hope that someone would pass who would be able to take proper care of him. People did come that way for shellfish and driftwood, but it seemed a long time before he heard the crunch of footsteps approaching. He turned, and saw two policemen. His heart gave a jump.

"What are you doing down there?" asked one. It was a habit with him to speak in an accusing tone.

"I'm taking care of my friend." Pinocchio sounded confused; he looked as if he had something to hide.

"What's the matter with him?" Pinocchio said nothing. Both men bent down and looked closely at the unconscious boy. "He's been hit on the head; did you do it?"

"No!"

"Here's the weapon," said the second policeman, picking up the Treatise which was lying on the sand. "Is this your book?"

"Yes, but—"

"Come along, then." They each took an arm of the puppet, and hauled him to his feet. "No, don't go on about being innocent; you're wasting your breath. You can tell us all about it later. Hey, you!" the first policeman shouted to a fisherman who had appeared at the far end of the beach with a shrimping net. "We're leaving this wounded boy with you; take him home, will you, and look after him? We'll be back tomorrow.

Now then, get a move on!" he ordered, jabbing Pinocchio with his elbow, and the three marched briskly away.

Poor Pinocchio felt he was in a nightmare. Even when he was allowed to speak, what could he say in his own defence? Who would believe him? But worst of all, he knew that when they went through the village, they would pass the fairy's house. She would be waiting for him to come home from school, she would look out of the window, she would see him walking past between two policemen. This thought was like a thorn in his heart.

Just as they were coming into the village, a squall of wind caught his cap and blew it off his head.

"Oh – my cap, my cap! Please, can I run and get it?"

"Very well, but no tricks! Hurry up!"

The cap was lying in the gutter, just a stone's throw away. The policemen thought they could safely let Pinocchio go that little distance, but they didn't know how fast he could run. He dodged down, snatched up the cap, and dashed on, heading back towards the sea.

The policemen blew their whistles and waved their arms, but they knew they would never catch up with him. So they sent one of their dogs – a mastiff called Alidoro, who was the fastest dog on the island, and an expert at catching criminals.

Alidoro ran like the wind after Pinocchio. Soon the puppet could hear him panting behind him, and feel his hot, fierce breath. So he swerved away from the beach and leapt up a rocky headland, which was closer, and jumping from boulder to boulder, plunged in the nick of time into the sea.

Now Alidoro was in trouble, because he couldn't swim. He wanted to stop, but his own speed carried him on, and with a mighty *splosh*! he joined Pinocchio in the waves. Blobbing back up to the surface with his mouth full of sea water, he tried desperately to keep afloat, but the harder he paddled, the more he went under. At last he threw back his head and howled, "Help me! Help me, Pinocchio, or I shall be drow-wow-wowned! Help help! Wow wow! Help! Wow!"

At first Pinocchio thought, It serves him right! But really he was very kind-hearted, and soon he took pity on the struggling beast. He shouted, "If I help you, will you promise to leave me alone, and not chase me any more?"

"I promise! I promise!" cried Alidoro pathetically, his last word swallowed in a string of bubbles. So Pinocchio caught him by the tail, and towed him to shore, and left him to recover; for the poor animal was so full of sea water, that he was swollen like a barrel, and he sprawled on the sand, gasping and blinking like a stranded fish.

CHAPTER TWELVE

In which the puppet swims to safety, but is caught by a sea green man monster. How he escapes being fried, and goes back to the fairy's house. How he has to wait too long for a snail, and faints at last from hunger and exhaustion.

Pinocchio swam on, keeping close to the shore, until he had covered a considerable distance. Now he thought he would be safe, and looked about him for a suitable landing place, and presently spied a large cave among the rocks, with a plume of smoke issuing from it. There must be a fire in that cave, he thought. What luck! I'll be able to warm and dry myself; I could probably spend the night there.

So he started swimming towards the rocks. Imagine his surprise, when what he had believed to be the sea bed, suddenly lifted up under him, and he found himself trapped in an enormous net! It was full of fish, all flapping and jumping as if they were crazy. He tried to escape, but he wasn't quick enough, for someone was hauling in the net. It was a fisherman, but he was so ugly that he looked more like a sea monster. He

was all covered with green scales, and instead of hair, a bush of green leaves sprouted from his head, and a beard of green weed grass draggled down almost to the ground.

"Bravo! I shall feast today as if it was my birthday!" the monster fisherman exclaimed, hauling away, and grinning as he eyed his catch.

Good for you, and good for me that I'm not a fish, thought Pinocchio, trying to keep up his spirits.

The fisherman pulled the net right out of the sea, and bumped it over the rocks in a manner very painful to its occupants. His cave was dank and dark and full of smoke; there was a fire in the middle, with a great frying pan on it, full of boiling oil. Beyond the constant lapping of the waves, the oil hissed, and something drip, drip, dripped at the back of the cave.

"Now let's see what we got!" cried

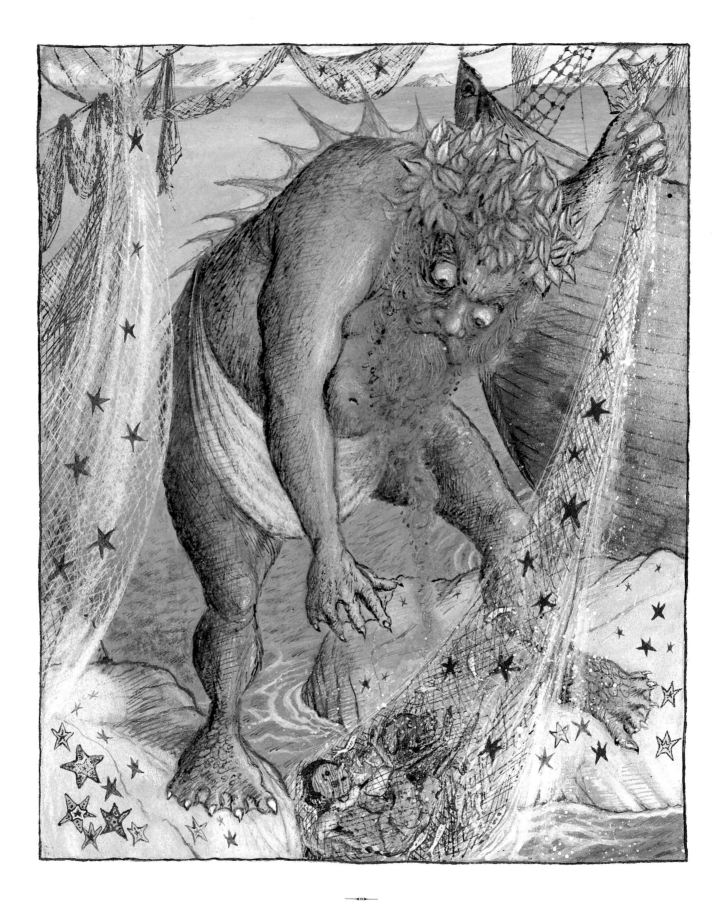

"I shall eat you all right, and you won't hurt me. I've eaten all category of fish from dabs to congers, and never a one as hurt me – don't you worry your little puppet head 'bout that. Dear little sole," said the monster, holding Pinocchio tightly and sprinkling him with a mixture of pepper and flour, and lifting him up to drop him in the pan of oil—

Exactly at that moment, a large mastiff darkened the entrance to the cave. He had picked up the glorious scent of cooking oil from far away, and now he rushed in, wagging his tail and howling with hunger.

"Get out!" roared the green monster. "Get out or I'll kick you out – you blubberous 'uge walrush you!"

But the dog was too famished to care what he said or did. He was about to snatch a meal from the net, when he heard a familiar voice. "Alidoro, Alidoro, save me, or I shall be fried!"

The dog looked up, and recognized Pinocchio all white with flour as he was, and helpless in the fisherman's grasp. He jumped up and grabbed him, and tore out of the cave, holding the puppet safely between his jaws. The fisherman gave a bellow of rage, and unhooked his trident to hurl at the fugitives, but by that time they were out of sight.

Alidoro ran all the way to the road

the green fisherman. His words came out oddly, as if his tongue was slow, or too big for his mouth. He stared into the net with his luminous, light-green eyes, and pulled out – Pinocchio! He held him close to his face, and frowned, and stared, with his mouth open and two stumpy teeth showing.

"What's this? What's this?" he said slowly. "Never did I see any fish like it! Or is it a crab? Yes, I do believe that's what it is – a crab!"

"I'm not a crab!" shouted Pinocchio. "I'm a puppet!"

"Puppet? What's that, a *puppet* fish? I never tasted a *puppet* fish! I do eat dog fishes, and very good they be, but I never so much as 'eared of a *puppet* fish!"

"I'm not a fish at all, and you can't eat me – I'll give you a terrible pain!"

which led to the village, and there he stopped, and set Pinocchio gently down.

Pinocchio patted his rough coat, and looked at him most gratefully. "How can I ever thank you?"

"No need – one good turn deserves another!"

They walked on together a little way, and then Alidoro raced ahead to his kennel at police headquarters; but Pinocchio had seen the fisherman who had been told to care for the injured boy. He wanted news of him, before he returned to the village. He went over to talk to him with an anxiously beating heart.

"He's not here any more," the fisher-

man said, knocking out his pipe on the end of the bench where he was sitting.

"Dead?" faltered Pinocchio.

"*Dead?* Bless you, no – not a bit of it! He had a rest here, and a glass of milk, and then he went home as right as rain!"

This was the best news Pinocchio could have. "That's wonderful!" he cried.

"Mind you, it was a nasty blow. You look as if you've been in trouble yourself. Lord, how you smell of fish! Why are you so white?"

"Oh, it's nothing," said Pinocchio with a blush. He wasn't going to say he'd nearly been fried like a haddock!

"Are you going home in that state? If I had a change of clothes I'd give it to you. Here! Take this cotton bag I keep beans in." And the kindly fisherman cut holes for his head and arms, and rolled his dirty clothes into a bundle. Then Pinocchio set off for the village.

But now he began to feel more and more ashamed. Here I am, dressed in an old bean bag! he thought. What's the fairy going to say? She'll be cross with me, that's certain. She may send me away. Oh dear! I can't bear it if she's angry! I'd sooner go away now, and travel the world, and keep kind memories of her!

But then he thought, *Travel the world* – what will happen then? I'm sure to do wrong, whether I mean it or not, and then I'll end up in prison, or on the end of a rope. No! It's better to go home, and

tell her I'm sorry, and when she scolds me, I'll have to put up with it. I deserve it, anyway!

So he argued in his thoughts, to and fro, to and fro, and now it was getting dark. Sometimes he walked on, sometimes he went back; he couldn't make up his mind. At last he found himself in front of the fairy's house. By this time it was night, and blowing a gale. No lights were showing, she must have gone to bed; but he knew she would let him in. He raised his hand to the knocker – and then he was suddenly afraid, and ran away. Then he came creeping back, in the dark and the wind and the rain, and he did knock, but he was so nervous, that he only tapped very lightly. He waited; he waited a long time.

At last a glow appeared in the attic, right up under the roof. He saw a snail up there, carrying a tiny light on her head. She opened the window, and called down, "Is anyone there?"

"Yes, it's me," whispered Pinocchio, with his teeth chattering. "I'm the pup-pup-puppet who lives with the fair-fair-fairy. Is she at ho-ho-home?"

"She's in bed," said the snail, who spoke as she moved, very slowly. "You mustn't disturb her. Wait there, I'll come down and let you in."

"Oh please hurry! I'm so cold and wet!" But she had gone; the window was shut, the light extinguished.

Time passed – one hour – two hours. It was raining so hard that the village street looked like a river. Pinocchio was just about to knock gently again when he saw the little light at a bedroom window.

"Oh please, dear snail!" he cried. "Come down quick, and open the door!"

"I am a snail, and I move at a snail's pace. Have patience." And the window snapped shut, the light disappeared.

Another hour passed – another two hours. Pinocchio suddenly lost his temper. What right had that sluggish snail to keep him standing in the cold and wet on his own doorstep? He seized the knocker in a rage – but to his astonishment it turned into an eel which slipped from his grasp and escaped in the rain water pouring down the street. Then Pinocchio dashed at the door, and gave it a kick that should have smashed it to splinters, but instead his foot went clean through the wood and he couldn't get it back. He struggled and cried – it was useless! He shouted, but nobody came. He had to spend the rest of that night lying in a puddle with his foot clamped firmly in the door.

At dawn, he heard a key turning in the lock, and bolts being slowly drawn back. It was the snail, who always kept her word, and had got down at last to let him in.

"What are you doing there? You've broken the door!"

"It was an accident. Please help me!" gasped the puppet, quite worn out. "I don't know what the fairy will say."

"She'll be sorry for me, I know she will, if you tell her how wet and cold and hungry and miserable I am!"

"She's asleep, and mustn't be disturbed," said the snail.

"At least you might bring me some food. She wouldn't want me to starve on her doorstep!"

"We'll see," said the snail, severely, and she went away.

Several hours later she returned, carrying a silver tray which she put down beside the puppet. There was a roast chicken on the tray, some fresh bread, and four ripe apricots.

"The fairy has sent you some breakfast," said the snail, and she went back into the house.

Now Pinocchio had been ready to die from hunger and grief, but when he saw the tray, he felt better at once. He picked out an apricot and bit into it. Alas! It wasn't a fruit at all – it was made of painted plaster! He was filled with despair, and tried to throw away the tray and everything on it, but the effort was too great – he fell back in a faint on the ground.

CHAPTER THIRTEEN

In which Pinocchio renews his good resolutions, and keeps them so well that the fairy says he will turn into a real boy that very night! Alas! He listens to bad advice, and takes the coach with all the other silly, idle children, and is whirled away to Playland!

When he woke, he was lying on his own bed inside the house, and the fairy was sitting beside him.

"My dear little Pinocchio, you suffer too much," she said sadly. "You do something wrong — and look what happens! All these dreadful adventures!"

"I know — I know," he groaned. "I shall never be a real boy!" Hot tears ran down his wooden cheeks, and spilt on to the pillow.

"Rubbish! You have to try harder, that's all! Learn from your mistakes, and don't listen to bad advice. Keep in good company — work hard at school — and in the end you'll win your heart's desire!"

"That can't be true," he sobbed. "Something always goes wrong to spoil it!"

The fairy patted his hand to comfort him. "It *is* the truth," she said. "You'll see! But you *must* keep your part of the bargain."

Pinocchio felt suddenly hopeful. Something in her voice made him believe that, being a fairy, she could see into the future.

"Do you promise?" he asked, sniffing, and wiping his face on the quilt.

"Yes."

"Then I promise to do my best from now on. I truly will."

"I know you will," she said.

This conversation made a deep impression on Pinocchio. It gave him strength and courage, and he had had so many bad frights, that he really did seem to change his character. He behaved so well, and worked so hard, that no-one could find any fault with him — except the badly-behaved, lazy boys, and now he didn't listen to them. But he didn't think much of himself — oh no! He remembered too clearly all the foolish mistakes he'd made.

As time went on, he longed more and more to be real. Every evening he looked hopefully at the fairy, without daring to mention it. But at last, the great day came when she suddenly announced, "Tomorrow we are going to have a party!"

"Hooray!" cried Pinocchio, who had just come home from school. "What sort of party? Who for?"

"For you. My dear Pinocchio, tomorrow you will go to bed a puppet, and next morning, when you wake up, you will be a real boy!"

Pinocchio's face turned scarlet with excitement. His heart began beating wildly. "That's wonderful! Oh! I didn't think it would ever happen! And a party to celebrate! Can I invite everyone in my class? Can I invite everyone in the whole school?"

"Of course you can! You can invite whoever you like, and I shall make hundreds of cakes and sausage rolls, and jugs and jugs of everything anyone could possibly want to drink!"

"I'd better go now and tell them about it!"

"Yes, you must. But be sure to come home before dark."

"I will; I'll be back in an hour!"

He gave her a kiss, and dashed down the street, turning cartwheels as he went. His heart was ready to burst

with happiness. At last – at last his wish was going to come true! What could spoil it now?

Pinocchio spread his invitations far and wide – it looked as if the whole village was coming to his party! But there was one boy he couldn't find, although he called at his house several times. He was the laziest, naughtiest boy in the class, always cracking jokes or making fun of the schoolmaster. Lessons were certainly brighter when he was there, and for this reason, and because he was very tall and thin, he was nicknamed Lampwick. Everyone liked him, and Pinocchio was particularly anxious to have him at the party.

He searched for him all through the village, and found him at last curled up in somebody's woodshed. "What on earth are you doing in here?" he asked in surprise. "Can you come to my party tomorrow?"

"What party's this?"

"It's a celebration, because tomorrow night, I'm going to turn into a real boy!"

"Huh!" said Lampwick, unimpressed.

"Don't you think that's wonderful?" demanded Pinocchio, creeping in beside him.

"I'm glad *you* think so! Much good may it do you – I shan't be there to see."

"What do you mean? Are you going somewhere?"

"I'm off to a marvellous country – believe me, a real dream place! It's called Playland – haven't you heard of it?"

"No—"

"Well then, imagine this! No lessons, no homework, no teachers! No scolding, no punishments! Nothing to do but have fun all day! Doesn't it sound ideal for boys like us? The holidays start on New Year's Day and go on till after Christmas. The only days in the week are Saturdays and Sundays. Oh, I can't wait!"

Pinocchio's eyes were shining at the thought of this fabulous country. "I never heard of anything like it. How do you get there?"

"There's a coach tonight – it'll stop here for me as soon as it's dark."

"And you're leaving – just like that? Aren't you afraid to go there alone? What if the whole thing's a joke? What if this ideal country of yours doesn't really exist?"

"It exists all right, and I shan't be alone – the coach is always packed. Why don't you join us and see for yourself?"

"I can't do that – of course I can't! – What sort of fun do you have in a place like that?"

"I don't know – it's all laid on – anything you want! Come along and find out!"

The thought was exceedingly tempting – almost irresistible – but

Pinocchio shook his head. "No. I can't."

"Stay and see the coach come, anyhow. It'll be here before long."

Pinocchio looked out, and saw to his dismay that it was already getting dark. The fairy would be waiting for him.

"I'd better go," he said, scrambling to his feet. "I'm late as it is; they'll be worrying at home."

"Tut tut! Are they afraid the bats will eat you?"

"No, but all the same—"

"Let them worry; who cares? Haven't you got a mind of your own? Don't you think it's your duty to wave good-bye to your old school friend, when probably we'll never see each other again?"

If that was true, perhaps it was a good enough excuse. The puppet settled back beside Lampwick. He had the greatest curiosity to see the coach

"Not any school at *all*?" he said. It was difficult to believe. Now he had won his wish – or almost won it – he did feel that he had a great deal of schoolwork.

"Nothing! Just fun, and fun, and fun, all day, every day!"

"But won't you get bored?"

"Of course not! If it was boring, it wouldn't be fun!"

Pinocchio hugged his knees, imagining the joys of Playland, and both boys were silent for a while.

Now it was quite dark. Suddenly they heard the tinkling of little bells, and the muffled hoot of a horn like the buzz of a wasp. Then a dim light showed in the distance, moving towards them, and presently the coach appeared.

Lampwick was right – it was packed with children, their heads crammed the windows. Its wheels were swaddled with rags, and it was drawn by a string of donkeys wearing white leather boots, two pairs each, to stop their hooves from clattering. These

donkeys were all different – white, grey, brown, spotted – and even striped in gay colours. It made Pinocchio smile just to look at them, they seemed so jolly. Playland must be a cheerful place, he thought. It must be a wonderful place, a beautiful, marvellous place – "Are you sure there are holidays all week, all year long?" he asked wistfully, aloud.

"Yes, yes! Quite sure!" cried voices from the coach. Lampwick didn't answer; he was climbing up to the box by the coachman, because there was no room for him inside.

"How about you, dear lad?" said the coachman, bending down to the puppet with a flattering smile. "Don't you want to come with us to Playland?" He was a short man with a pot belly and shiny scarlet cheeks. He had very bright eyes and a tight little mouth that looked as if it wanted to laugh, not too kindly perhaps.

"Well, I do, but I can't," said Pinocchio, stroking the neck of one of the donkeys. To his surprise, it suddenly kicked out, and he found himself spreadeagled on a heap of stones. Everyone in the coach, and Lampwick, and the coachman, burst out laughing.

"Come along," said the coachman, wiping the laugh off his face, and reaching down to Pinocchio. "We can make room for you on the box – if you aren't happy, you know, you can go home at once."

"Do you mean that?"

"Of course! That's what Playland is – the only country in the world where everybody has a good time *all* the time!"

The children inside the coach clapped and cheered when they heard this, and Lampwick said, "What are you waiting for? He's told you you can walk out if you don't like it!"

Poor Pinocchio was in torment, he was so tempted. I'll go straight home, he thought to himself, as soon as I've seen it, and the fairy will be so interested to hear about it, because it must be such a good and lovely place.

While he was making up his mind he was automatically scratching the neck of another of the donkeys, when he noticed with horror that there were tears in its eyes, and heard it say in a low voice, "Don't listen to them, you fool! I did, and look what's become of me!"

"Mr Coachman," cried Pinocchio, "this donkey of yours can speak!"

"Some of my beasts are very gifted," the coachman replied with a buttery smile. "They only talk nonsense, however – don't listen to him. Well, come if you're coming; we can't wait for you all night!"

Then Pinocchio put his foot on the step, and eager arms reached out to help him up; he squeezed into the space beside Lampwick, the coachman cracked his whip, and the coach bowled noiselessly away.

CHAPTER FOURTEEN

*The pleasures of Playland, in which Lampwick and Pinocchio enjoy
themselves very much, until they turn into donkeys! How Pinocchio glimpses
the fairy at the circus, and soon after injures himself performing in the ring.*

It was a long, long journey to Playland, and when at last the coach stopped in the centre of the city, Pinocchio and Lampwick tumbled off half-asleep, and stared round them with astonishment. Children were playing everywhere, with balls, bicycles, skittles, hoops, and every game ever invented; they were running, jumping, hopping, sliding, climbing, skipping; they were laughing, clapping, chanting, shouting, whistling and singing. The streets were lined with toy shops, clothes shops, sports shops. There were theatres and a circus which showed a different programme every day, and there was an enormous fun fair, with a giant dipper so high that its top was lost in the clouds. Best of all, in the city park, a mock battle was going on, where everyone had a chance to shoot and smash things up and nobody got hurt.

What joy! even if the noise was deafening, even if the walls of every building were covered in graffiti, and the streets were full of litter because it was no fun to pick it up! Every child clutched a snack or a sweet, every face was sticky and smiling. The coachman seemed to be the only adult in Playland, and he had gone off with his coach and his multi-coloured donkeys. Lampwick and Pinocchio looked about amazed, while the glory of the place gradually dawned on them, and then they started grinning from ear to ear. Poor fairy! Pinocchio didn't give her a thought! He couldn't wait to try the dipper; he thumped Lampwick on the shoulder, and the two rushed off in different directions to enjoy themselves.

So this was how the puppet lived for days – weeks – months. A beautiful life! A wonderful life! Whenever he met Lampwick, he thanked him for leading

him to Playland, and they agreed that they were perfectly happy – happier than they had ever been!

But then the morning came when Pinocchio woke up with a headache, and a hot feeling in his ears, and the more he rubbed them, the hotter and the odder they felt. They seemed to be swelling rapidly. He rolled off the bed and stumbled across the room to the mirror. Here he examined first one ear, then the other; and what he saw made his heart beat uncomfortably. His ears were growing longer – longer – and longer – and they were covered in soft brown fur!

Pinocchio burst into tears. He tried to pull off those tell-tale ears, and shouted for Lampwick, and he made so much noise that a squirrel who lived on the floor above came hurrying down, and tapped on his door.

"What's the matter, dear neighbour?"

"Oh I'm sick – I'm terribly, terribly sick!"

The squirrel came in and looked at him, and said, "Dear me! Oh my poor friend, I'm afraid I have bad news for you! You've got donkey disease."

"What's that?" cried the puppet, while his heart turned cold with dread.

"It means that soon you won't be a puppet any more. You'll have turned into a common donkey, such as you see everywhere, loaded with sacks, or patiently grinding corn, or pulling carts to market—"

"But I don't want to be a donkey!" screamed Pinocchio, beside himself with fright.

"It's too late now," said the calm squirrel. "This is what happens to all the children who leave school, and run away from home, and don't trouble to learn anything or improve themselves. Look at this dirty, untidy little room, and I don't expect you've washed your face since you've been here. You've done nothing but please yourself, morning, noon and night. Of course you're a donkey! What else could you be?"

"It's all Lampwick's fault!" wept Pinocchio. "I didn't want to come – he made me! Oh – I'll get even with him!" He wanted to rush out immediately, but first he found a large cap to cover his ears, for he was afraid of being laughed at. Then he hunted through all the delights of Playland, but he couldn't find Lampwick anywhere. At last he went to his lodging, and leaning on the bell, he banged on the knocker.

"Who is it?"

"Me – Pinocchio!"

"Wait there – I'll come in a minute."

It was several minutes however before Lampwick opened the door, and to the puppet's surprise, he too was wearing a large cap that completely covered his head! What did this mean? Perhaps he had the donkey disease!

The boys looked at each other. Pinocchio was the first to break the silence.

"Why are you wearing that cap, Lampwick?"

"No special reason – I'm cold, that's all – got a cold in my head. Why are you wearing yours?"

"Oh – same thing."

"Have you got earache?" asked Pinocchio, after another silence.

"No – yes, a bit – nothing particular – what about you?"

"Nothing special."

They stared at each other's caps without speaking for a while.

"Lampwick," said Pinocchio, "I wish you'd take that cap off. We're old friends, after all."

"Well, I might – if you do."

"All right – go on, then!"

"And you – on the count of three!"

One – two – *three!* The caps came off, and both boys burst out laughing. They did look so comical to each other with donkey ears!

But suddenly Lampwick turned pale, and cried out, "Oh – oh! Help me, oh help! Pinocchio!"

"What's wrong?" exclaimed Pinocchio in terror.

"I can't stand up! My back's breaking!"

There was nothing the puppet could do to help him, or himself either for that matter. Within minutes both boys were running round the room on all fours. Their faces grew long and hairy, their hands and feet hardened into hooves, and they were soon covered with warm brown donkey coats. Last of all, their tails began to grow. At this most humiliating moment, they put up their heads, and – brayed. No words

came out – only hideous noise! The change was complete, and at that moment, somebody hammered on the door.

"Let me in! You know me, I'm the coachman who brought you here. Open up!"

As neither boy moved, he kicked the door in, and stood looking at them, smiling and rubbing his hands. This wicked little man tempted foolish children and brought them to Playland, so that when they turned into donkeys he could sell them for a good price. In this way he had amassed a large fortune.

"How well you bray!" he exclaimed. He took a brush and comb out of his pocket, and groomed Pinocchio and Lampwick until their coats shone like satin. Then he put scarlet halters on them, and led them away to market.

———◦———

Lampwick was sold first, and taken away – who knows where? Pinocchio was bought by an animal trainer, who wanted him to dance in a circus. He had to learn to jump through a paper hoop, and waltz, and polka, and stand on his hind legs. He got enough to eat – if hay and straw could ever be enough for a donkey who had kept his human appetite. His master was kind, and gave him a bowl of oats on Sundays, and apples whenever he performed well. Pinocchio did his best, but his heart was

full of grief. How he would have loved to learn to dance in his puppet shape, but how difficult it was now!

But at last huge coloured posters appeared all through the town, advertising a Grand Full-Dress Performance by all the artistes and horses of the company, *including* the LITTLE DONKEY PINOCCHIO, STAR OF THE DANCE. The show was immediately sold out! The tent was packed with boys and girls all eager to see this famous donkey! The circus band played a stirring tune, and when Pinocchio trotted into the ring, the applause was tremendous!

He was wearing a brand new bridle of shiny painted leather, with buckles and studs of polished brass. Instead of a saddle, he had a broad band of glittering silver and gold fixed round his body. White flowers had been fastened behind his ears, his mane had been curled and decorated with silk ribbons, and crimson and blue velvet ribbons were plaited into his tail. The ringmaster, too, looked magnificent in his black coat, white breeches, and black leather boots long enough to cover his knees. He had waxed his moustaches until they stuck out like the handlebars on a bicycle. He carried a shiny top hat in one hand, and a long whip in the other.

For the moment, Pinocchio forgot his troubles. All these people had come

to see him! This clapping and cheering was for him! Suddenly he felt on top of the world – proud, excited, determined to make his act a triumph!

The ringmaster cracked his whip. "Now, Pinocchio!" he cried, in his fierce, hoarse voice. "Salute this distinguished company!"

Pinocchio trotted obediently to the centre of the arena, bowed his head, and knelt down. Everyone shouted and cheered.

After a minute, the ringmaster cracked his whip again, and shouted, "Walk!"

The donkey got up and walked in a spirited manner round the ring.

"Trot!"

"Gallop!"

Then, while he was racing round the ring as fast as he could go, the ringmaster drew a pistol, and fired it into the air. Bang! The performing donkey stopped dead in mid-gallop and crumpled up on the ground, as if he had been shot.

Some of the audience screamed, some cheered, and everyone clapped – the tent was so noisy, the circus band was inaudible.

As Pinocchio got to his feet in this tumult of applause, he raised his eyes to the spectators, and saw, in the middle of the front row, a beautiful lady with long blue hair. She was wearing a medallion on a gold chain round her neck, and on it was the portrait of a puppet!

Pinocchio was overcome with astonishment and joy. It's the fairy, he thought, the dear fairy! She must have forgiven me, if she's wearing my picture round her neck! He couldn't believe it, and yet it was true – there she sat, looking at him as if she could see through the donkey skin to the puppet inside. Oh how kindly she looked at him! His heart was so full of happiness that he shouted, "Oh my dear fairy!" – but the words were lost. The only sound that came out was a donkey's ugly bray, and some of the smallest children were so frightened that they burst into tears.

"Come, come – that's not allowed in polite society!" exclaimed the ring-master, and he gave the donkey a tap on the nose with his whip that made his eyes water. Alas! when he looked again, the seat was empty, the fairy had gone.

Poor Pinocchio was overcome with despair. But he had to go on with his performance – even now the ringmaster was cracking his whip and holding out the paper hoop. Pinocchio galloped towards it, but his spirits had gone. Three times he lost courage at the last moment and ran underneath without jumping. At the fourth attempt he leapt, but he caught one of his hind legs and fell heavily to the ground. When he struggled up, he was lame, and could hardly walk the short distance back to his stable.

CHAPTER FIFTEEN

*In which Pinocchio is bought for fifty pence by a wicked old man who wants
to make a drum out of his skin. How he is saved from drowning and his
donkey shape by a shoal of fish. How he struggles to rescue a little blue goat,
when an enormous shark swallows him! How he surprises Geppetto at dinner!*

There was consternation in the circus tent, but that didn't help Pinocchio. Neither did the cards and presents that were delivered to his stable. His leg didn't get any better, and when the vet saw it, his verdict was grim. Pinocchio the Dancing Donkey would be lame for the rest of his life.

"Sorry, old chap," said the ringmaster, patting his neck and giving him a carrot. "I'm afraid you'll have to go — we can't afford to keep a donkey who will never work again!"

Pinocchio knew that this was true. He hung his head, and limped away with the stable boy. He didn't think anyone would want him now, but he was wrong. A swarthy old man approached the boy and offered him fifty pence for the lame donkey. The boy was glad to take it, and Pinocchio found himself with a new owner.

This old man was a maker of musical instruments, and sad to say, he had bought the donkey because he had to make a drum for the town band, and he needed a skin. He led Pinocchio to a rocky place on the seashore, where he found a large boulder, which he roped to his neck. Pinocchio stood patiently while the old man made these preparations. He said to himself, Courage! I have been in tight places before, and come through. I am not dead yet. And he thought about his dear father, and how the fairy had promised that they would meet again; and then he thought about the fairy, her beautiful hair, and his picture in gold round her neck. The hungry sea slapped at the rocks; from the colour of it he could tell that it was deep. Courage! he thought. My story will have a happy ending! And he shut his eyes, just as the horrid old man cried, "Over you go!" and gave him a push.

Pinocchio the donkey fell down,

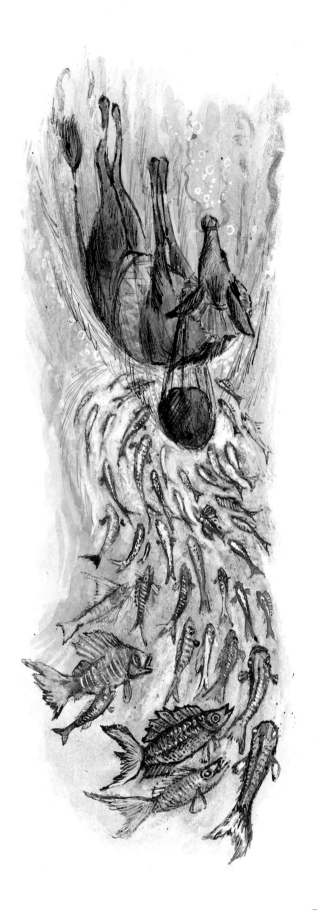

down, down. He had no chance of swimming with that weight round his neck. The old instrument maker sat on the rocks and smoked, keeping his foot on the end of the rope. Time passed; after about an hour he started hauling in, expecting to see a dead donkey come wallowing up to the surface. Not a bit of it! Imagine his rage and astonishment, when he found a wooden puppet on the end of his line! A wooden puppet, surrounded by a shoal of fish who burst out laughing when they saw the infuriated old man!

The fish had rushed at the donkey when he fell helplessly into the water. The fairy had sent them, and they gobbled him up in large mouthfuls, until only his wooden skeleton was left. *That* was the puppet! Pinocchio was himself once more, and very glad to be rid of his donkey disguise!

"What about my fifty pence?" roared the nasty old man. "I'll get even with you! I'll sell you for firewood, you cheat! You swindler!"

But Pinocchio had already untied the rope from his neck, and with a joyful farewell wave, he struck out for the open sea. Today it was very blue, reflecting the sky where little clouds were scudding like the waves that tossed him playfully about. He swam for the pleasure of it, not caring where he was going, until he saw just ahead of him a rock that looked as if it was made of white marble. A goat was standing on top of it, a beautiful little goat with a blue fleece, who began bleating piteously when she noticed him in the water. Pinocchio swam towards her, using his fastest stroke. His heart was beating hard, for the blue of the goat was exactly the colour of the fairy's hair!

But just as he was approaching the marble rock – just as he was about to give an encouraging shout – something terrible happened. An immense shark, the size of a five-storey apartment block, suddenly loomed on the horizon; and when he spotted the puppet with his dreadfully sharp eyes, he dashed directly at him! All Pinocchio heard was a swishing noise, and he looked round – straight into the gape of an immense mouth, which was easily big enough for a railway train including the smoke, and armed with three rows of pointed teeth! There was no time to dodge – the shark gulped him down without a hiccup. The poor puppet found himself slurping about in the inky blackness of the monster's stomach, up to his knees in evil-smelling water. This was the most miserable accident, to escape from certain death by drowning, only to be swallowed and digested! He began to cry bitterly.

"What is the matter?" a deep twanging voice presently inquired, close to his ear.

Pinocchio nearly overbalanced with fright, and the sobs stuck in his throat. "Who's there?" he croaked.

"I am a tunny fish," the ponderous voice replied, "and I am awaiting my fate with the laudable fortitude peculiar to my class."

As the puppet didn't know what laudable meant, or fortitude either, he was silent.

He noticed that the atmosphere in the huge stomach was not as foul as might have been expected. The shark was very old. He suffered from asthma and palpitations, so that he had to breathe through his mouth, and regular draughts of fresh air relieved the congestion. Also, the blackness of his stomach was not as inky as it had seemed at first. There was even a glimmer of light ahead, perhaps a quarter of a mile distant, but Pinocchio hesitated to ask the tunny about it, for every now and then the creature heaved a sigh as if the melancholy of the situation was almost too much to bear. At last, overcome by curiosity, he said goodbye timidly to the fish, and began splashing his way towards the light, which brightened steadily as he approached. He waded on, and waded on, and at last he came on a strange scene.

There was a table covered with a white cloth, lit by a candle which had been stuck in a bottle. The table was set with a cup and plate; on the plate were two biscuits, a sliver of cheese, and a

sugared orange, while the cup was almost full of sparkling wine. A little old man was sitting at the table. He wore a wig of yellow curly hair, which made an odd contrast with his long white beard.

When Pinocchio looked that old man in the face, he gave a great cry of joy and astonishment.

"Daddy! It's you, it is, it is! Oh Daddy, my dear, dear Daddy!"

It was indeed Geppetto, and he peered at Pinocchio, and then he started to smile. His kind old face creased into a thousand wrinkles.

"My dear little Pinocchio!" he said. "And to think I had lost all hope of ever seeing you again!"

They sat side by side, clasping each other by the hand. First, Pinocchio had to tell the complete history of his adventures.

"But what about you?" he asked, when he had finished. "When I last saw you, you were out in your little boat on that stormy sea. What happened next?"

"Why, I sank, you know – and then I would have drowned, but this huge shark swallowed me whole. Then I would have starved, or anyway died of thirst, but by a miraculous chance he took in a merchant ship loaded with all sorts of provisions – preserved meat and fruit – cheese – wine – and as you see, matches and candles. So I've lived in here for I don't know how long, and really I've been remarkably comfortable,

or I would have been if I hadn't been worrying about you—" Pinocchio squeezed his hand. Geppetto cleared his throat, and went on, "That's all in the past, thank goodness. But now, my dear boy, our present trouble is this. Our stores have run out. This is the very last candle. This is the last of the food and wine, so we'd better share it, you know!"

Pinocchio was very glad of a biscuit, and half the cheese and orange. When he had gobbled them up, he said, "Daddy, we have to escape."

"True enough, my dear, but how?"

"There's only one way – through the shark's mouth! He has to open it whenever he takes a breath—"

"Is that so?" said the old man doubtfully, shaking his head. "Well, well. – But you know I can't swim."

"I can, I'm an excellent swimmer. You can ride on my back. You couldn't sink me if you tried!"

"You aren't very large—"

"Neither are you!"

The food had been eaten, the wine drunk, there was no reason to stay. Hand in hand, with Geppetto carrying the candle, they waded up the shark's stomach towards his jaws. By the light which flickered in the old man's hand, they could see a bizarre miscellany of swallowed goods bobbing around them – an icecream cart – a deckchair . . . All sorts of fish converged on them in a friendly fashion as they went along, tickling and nibbling at their legs.

The entrance to the stomach expanded as the shark breathed, or whenever he swallowed food and water which rushed in like a flood tide. Luckily for the fugitives, he was asleep at present; in fact, as they wormed their way through the rubbery aperture between stomach and throat, they were almost deafened by the thunder of his snores.

They tiptoed cautiously towards the echoing cavern of his mouth. His tongue lay ahead of them, as broad and long as a highway; beyond it curved the barrier of his teeth. They gripped each other's hands still more tightly as they made their way up the leathery tongue. Now between his half-open jaws they could see the calm night sky, luminous with the moon and stars; in the gaps between snores, they could hear the murmur of little waves outside. Freedom was so close!

CHAPTER SIXTEEN

*How Pinocchio and Geppetto escape out of the stomach of the monstrous
shark, and ride to safety on a tunny. How they encounter false friends from
long ago, and rediscover a true one. How they settle into a new home, and the
puppet begins to work hard for his living.*

Unfortunately, Geppetto was so frightened by the three rows of shark's teeth blocking the way, that his hand shook more than ever, and at the crucial moment he dropped the candle. The hot wax flew in all directions, and the sleeping monster came suddenly to life! First, he drew in his breath with a snort that bounced them against his tonsils – next, he gave a tremendous sneeze, that shot them out like bullets from a gun! Still clinging desperately to each other, they crashed into the sea five miles away, with a force that winded Geppetto and would certainly have drowned him, if Pinocchio hadn't been able to hoist him quickly on to his shoulders. Oh, he was exhausted himself, but he was so full of happiness he felt he could have carried twenty Geppettos to safety!

He scanned the horizon all ways, every way, but there was no land in sight, so he started swimming, hoping for the best. Geppetto was not optimistic. Pinocchio could feel him shivering, and he cried out, "Courage, dear Daddy! Keep a sharp look-out for land, so you can steer me in the right direction!"

"Land, land – where is this land?" muttered the old man, growing more and more uneasy as he looked for it in vain, and blinking like a sailor threading a needle. "All I can see is water and sky!"

"It will come, never fear!"

But Geppetto didn't believe it, and as time passed, Pinocchio too began to feel discouraged. He had to admit that he was almost exhausted, and if there was land ahead, it was questionable whether he would have the strength to reach it. At last he was so worn out that he could swim no further. He let himself float, and Geppetto squatted gloomily on top of him, while the sun rose, and the sea began to sparkle all round them

into the furthest distance.

"It's a beautiful day," said Pinocchio hopefully.

But all Geppetto could say was, "What will become of us now?"

What, indeed?

But at that moment, a plangent voice spoke close to the puppet's ear – a voice he recognized, like the twanging of an old guitar.

"Pinocchio!"

It was the sober tunny fish. He had watched the fugitives, and escaped from the shark by doing as they did. Full of gratitude, he had followed them faithfully, although he didn't understand why Pinocchio was swimming round and round in circles. At last he had come to the conclusion that they were in difficulties, and approached to offer his assistance.

"We're lost," Pinocchio told him, his eyes brimming with tears. "Even if I knew the way, I can't swim any more. We're done for!"

"Done for," Geppetto repeated, sadly shaking his head, and settling himself more securely on the puppet's body.

"Not so," the ponderous fish replied. "If you will but condescend to grasp my nethermost peduncle, or to put it another way, tail, I shall consider it my privilege to draw you anywhere you please; the nearest coast being but four minutes distant, swimming speedily."

"That's wonderful!" exclaimed Pinocchio. "But I'm afraid— Won't the weight of us drag you down?"

"Not in the slightest! Two empty cockleshells – no more."

So it was arranged, except that they had to climb upon the back of the tunny. He had a habit of gaily twitching his tail when cruising at speed, which made it impossible to hold.

Four minutes later he lowered himself against a sandy beach. Then Pinocchio clasped him with grateful arms, and pressed many kisses on his scaly cheeks. The tunny was so moved by this, that he slipped bashfully away into the tide, in case anyone noticed the tears in his goggle eyes.

"What are we going to do now?" asked Geppetto. He was leaning on Pinocchio's arm, so tired he was ready to drop.

The puppet knew no more than he did, but he made his voice cheerful. "We'll find shelter of some sort, so that you can rest. Don't worry – something will turn up!"

Geppetto said nothing, but he thought, I doubt it; and the corners of his mouth turned down, down towards the ground.

They had walked only a little way inland, when they came upon two beggars sitting on the bank. Pinocchio knew them at once, though they were greatly changed for the worse, and his heart skipped a beat. These were the fox and the cat, who had cost him such pain and grief, as well as all his money. The cat had lost both ears, and she had pretended to be blind for so long, that now her sight had gone. The fox was moth-eaten all down one side, and his brush was missing; however, he skipped out in front of the travellers with a cry of false friendship.

"Can it be – it is – yes, it *is* – Dear Pussy, our troubles are over!"

"Who is it?" growled the cat – she had lost her temper with her eyesight.

"Why, it's that charming, talented puppet we talk about so often, whose name for the moment escapes me – and he's brought his dear old father to see us—"

Pinocchio had nothing to give them, even if he wanted to; he walked on without saying anything. Presently he glanced back. The cat was spitting at him while the fox stood glowering in the middle of the road, shaking his fist.

"Friends of yours, my dear boy?" asked Geppetto, by and by.

"False friends, my dear Daddy."

The road took a turn downhill, which was fortunate, because otherwise Geppetto would have had to stop for a rest. It led into a valley, where there were pleasant fields and orchards, with a stream running through. Near the water's edge stood a little thatched cottage, with walls of red brick, and flowers and vegetables growing neatly in the front garden. Pinocchio hesitated; he glanced at his father; then he went boldly up the path and knocked on the door.

"Who is it?" asked a tiny creaking voice.

"Only a poor old man, and his son. We have nothing at all to eat, and nowhere at all to go!"

"If you turn the key you can open the door," squeaked the voice.

Pinocchio did so, and the two entered the house. They looked all round but the room seemed to be empty.

"Up here!" cried the voice, and they raised their eyes to the roof. Something small was glowing faintly on the cross beam, and as they stared at it, they made out the ghostly shape of the talking cricket.

Then Pinocchio trembled, but he thought to himself, It's no good, I shall have to apologize. So he called, "I say – cricket! I'm sorry I killed you with the hammer!"

"Well, well!" the tiny creature replied, sarcastically. "That was gracefully said; and now I suppose you want me to do you a good turn!"

"Not me – my poor daddy. May he rest here tonight at least?"

"He may stay as long as he likes – he's never done me any harm, and I shall enjoy a little conversation, when he feels up to it. There's some straw over there; you can pull it together for his bed."

Pinocchio made Geppetto as comfortable as he could, and the poor old man went gratefully to sleep. Then he called, in a hoarse whisper, "Please – cricket – "

"What now?"

"Where could I get him a cup of milk?"

"There's a farm up the road; they keep cows."

So Pinocchio ran to the farm, but he had no money to pay for milk; he had to agree to haul water. One hundred buckets he drew from the well for that one cup of milk – he had never worked so hard in his life!

Next day he went there again and worked for his milk – and the next day, and the next. He made himself useful in many ways. The farmer liked him because he was willing and cheerful, and he taught him how to weave baskets out of reed, which sold well at the market.

Geppetto was still weak and depressed, so to cheer him, the puppet made a little cart. He painted it yellow and blue, and on fine days he wheeled the old man out for a ride and a breath of fresh air. In the evenings, he practised reading and writing. He found an old book, and cut himself a pen out of a twig, and mixed ink from wild cherry and blackberry juice.

The three lived contentedly together, and Pinocchio paid for everything

– the others had no money. One day, he asked the cricket how he had managed to save up enough to buy the cottage.

"I didn't buy it. It was given to me."

"*Given?* What a gift! Whoever gave you such a wonderful gift?"

"A little blue goat. She said she couldn't live here any more; she ran down the road, bleating, bleating."

"A *blue* goat!" cried Pinocchio, and his heart began to pound. "Did she tell you where she was going?"

"No, she said nothing but bleat, bleat, bleat – but I could understand the meaning of it."

"Why, what did it mean?"

" 'Pinocchio, alas Pinocchio, the shark has swallowed you up!' "

"But that must have been the fairy – my own dear fairy!" cried the puppet in anguish, and he ran to ask the farmer whether he had seen her; but he hadn't, and he didn't believe in any such fairy tale creatures.

So that was that!

CHAPTER SEVENTEEN

In which Pinocchio sets off to market, but on the way he meets the snail. How he gives all his money for medicine for the blue-haired fairy. How the fairy comes to the puppet in his dream, and promises that he shall have his heart's desire. How the story of Pinocchio's adventures has a HAPPY ENDING!

What with one thing and another, Pinocchio worked so hard in all weathers that his clothes were scarcely fit to be seen. His coat and trousers were threadbare, his shoes worn through, and his cap was falling to bits. It took him a long time to save enough to get himself some new ones, but at last he ran along the road to the market with a fist full of coins, excitedly imagining the coat and shoes and trousers he would buy, and the cap with a feather in it.

Suddenly, he heard his name called, from the hedge.

He stopped in surprise, and looked round. Then he noticed a snail peering out at him. When she saw that she had caught his attention, she gradually approached, dragging her silvery trail.

"Don't you know me?"

"Well—" It would have been rude to say that one snail looked much like

another. She was certainly very fine.

"Don't you remember how I used to look after the lady with long blue hair? And how I rushed down to let you in when you came home in the middle of the night? And how you got your foot stuck in the door?"

"Yes, yes – of course I remember all that!" cried Pinocchio. "Tell me quickly, dear little snail – how is that beautiful lady? Is she well? Where is she? I long so much to see her!"

"But that I fear you can't," said the slow snail. "You see she's not well, not at all well – in fact, they've taken her to the hospital."

"*Hospital?*"

"Yes, and she's no better, and she's so wretchedly poor, she hasn't even a penny to pay for a bottle of medicine!"

"But that's dreadful! Something must be done immediately! Snail, dear snail – look – here is money – take it, take it all, at once, and hurry to the fairy! Don't wait a second – go your fastest – and now, we'll meet again here in a day or two, or three days perhaps if that's easier for you, and I'll have more money for you then. Keep it safe and run, snail, run!"

And strange to say, the snail ran off like a lizard.

When Pinocchio got home, rather pale, and out of breath, his father said, "What have you done with your new clothes?"

"Oh! I couldn't find anything I liked. Never mind – better luck next time!"

He was wretchedly anxious about the fairy. He couldn't eat any supper, and thought he wouldn't sleep a wink; but in fact he did fall asleep, as soon as his head touched the pillow. Then he had a wonderful dream.

He dreamt that the fairy was standing beside him. She bent down so that her long and blue and shining hair quite covered him, and she kissed him, and said, "Now, Pinocchio, I am going to give you your heart's desire. You deserve it, my dear, not because you never make mistakes, but because you have a truly loving heart."

"Don't go away," he begged in his dream. "Oh please – don't go away!" More than anything in the world, he longed for her to be with him always. And she did stay with him while he slept; but when he woke up, she vanished.

He opened his eyes. For some reason, his room seemed particularly bright this morning. He stared in astonishment. Instead of a clean but humble straw pallet, he had a nice little bed! He sat up and looked round. A chest of drawers, a mirror, a chair! On the chair, new clothes, neatly folded! Under the chair, a pair of leather boots!

He jumped out of bed, and caught sight of himself in the mirror. What was *this*? His eyes fixed on his reflection, his mouth fell open with amazement. Where was the round wooden head – the painted hair – the scarred, chipped features? He was looking at a handsome, unspoilt face, with thick brown hair, and kind, blue, sparkling eyes! His gaze moved downwards – he had hands! He had feet! He shouted with joy! He danced, he jumped over the bed, he turned somersaults and cartwheels – PINOCCHIO THE PUPPET WAS A REAL BOY AT LAST!

When he got dressed, he found a silver purse in his trouser pocket. These words were engraved upon it:

The blue-haired fairy returns Pinocchio's money and thanks him for his loving heart.

He opened the purse. Inside lay twenty pieces of shining gold!

He rushed in to Geppetto's room.

The old man was up early this morning. He had got out his tools and a piece of wood, and he was polishing his spectacles on his yellow wig. This was like old times! This was wonderful, wonderful! Even the talking cricket was a ghost no longer! He perched on Geppetto's work bench, recklessly close to the hammer, airing his philosophical opinions.

Then Pinocchio noticed something faded in the corner, propped awkwardly against a chair. The head had fallen forward, the arms dangled askew, the jointed legs bent at impossible angles – altogether it looked as if it was about to collapse on the ground. He walked across and tapped it on the head.

"You wait," he said. "You just wait and see what I'll do, now I'm a real boy!"